# RESCUE

Mac & Jennie – Book One

Gary Henderson

RealTime Library

RNWC Media, LLC

Book 1 in the series: Mac & Jennie

2nd Edition

Cover photographs: iStock.com/OSTILL

RNWC Media, LLC

PO Box 559, Pinehurst, TX 77362

https://RNWCMedia.com

https://MacAndJennie.com

Imprint: RNWC RealTime

Publisher's Note: This is a work of fiction. Names, characters, and incidents are a product of the author's imagination. Locales and public names are sometimes used for atmospheric purposes.

Book Layout adapted from Inspire © 2017 BookDesignTemplates.com

RESCUE / Gary Henderson --2nd ed.

ISBN 978-1-937975-27-2 print edition

ISBN 978-1-937975-38-8 electronic editions

# Dedication

To the One Who invites us to share in His creativity,

to those who have joined us in our writing fellowship,

and to my favorite editor, the one who said, "Yes."

Thank you.

# Preface

Welcome to RESCUE

Book 1 of the *Mac and Jennie* series.

* * *

Mac, longtime special ops veteran, and his new wife Jennie are hunted by longtime enemies, and lead the attackers on a long, dangerous chase across the country.

Back at Jennie's school her friend Celena writes code that pretends to predict stock prices.

When the fraud is discovered, Celena is thrown out of school and sent home to Venezuela.

Philip then re-writes the code as a big-data project that legitimately attempts to predict stock prices.

Leonard from Chicago wants that software. Leonard gets what he wants, and he takes Philip hostage.

Phillip's life will be short when Leonard finds that the software does not work.

Mac and Jennie are hired to protect Philip, and must rescue him... and Celena, now held hostage in Venezuela.

# Contents

# Chapter 1

Mac drifted down through the black sky, his parachute rippling in the crosswinds. Clouds hid the stars, and the moon forgot to come to the party.

Seventeen, eighteen, nineteen ... brace for it ...

Just before his feet hit the dirt, he could see enough to know which way the ground sloped, and managed to get through the fall with nothing broken. He struggled up, pulled his knife, and cut the cords away. Quickly rolling the chute up, he ran to the nearest line of trees, found some piled up leaves and branches, and buried it.

Now, he thought, breathing hard. Getting down alive. Check. Getting back alive ... hope that's on the list too!

Lifting the cover on the watch, he held it level and let the compass stop spinning.

That way. Half a mile?

Back out to the edge of the woods, he began moving along quietly, pausing behind trees now and then, listening and looking. A low plane would have drawn some attention. Had to get away from the drop spot quickly.

Voices ahead. Loud voices in the middle of the night. Flashlights waving. He turned into the woods and moved as far as he could before they got close enough to hear him.

The trees were dense, the mould thick. Years' worth of fallen leaves and twigs crunched softly under his step.

He chose a place surrounded by three trees and partly covered by a bush. He knelt down, tunneled into the topsoil as far as he could reach, then backed in and covered himself to leave only his eyes exposed, and a little path for air.

For two days he lay there, with soldiers passing frequently and sometimes close enough to smell his sweat. When things were quiet, he ate bits of chocolate, and when that was gone, whatever crawled close enough to be caught.

On the third night there were no soldiers. He eased out of the muck, brushed off what he could, and silently returned to the tree line, trying to get his leg muscles to work again.

How far? A few hundred yards?

A crescent moon rose behind the trees, throwing its pale light across the field beside him, but leaving him hidden in deep shadow. Fog was creeping into the valley.

The house appeared before him. Two men stood outside, one with a lit cigarette, both leaning against the house on the moonlit side, looking at the sky.

Blinded to me, Mac thought. I like their strategy.

He moved closer, staying in the shadows of the trees, slowly, slowly approaching.

A truck pulled up to the other side of the house, and the men walked out to meet it. Mac ran to the building, his sound hidden a bit by the rumbling diesel engine of the newcomer. A window on the side away from the men offered a view, and a small light bulb showed a man lying on a cot.

Mac tapped once, then twice, then once.

The man stood up, turned off the light, and came to the window. Mac opened his fold-up tool and held the mini flashlight on for a moment. Two Phillips-head screws held the bar across the window, and they had been put in carelessly. He spun the screws out and set the bar on the wet ground. The prisoner unlatched the simple, single pane window from the inside, pushed it up, climbed through, and looked about.

"Ben?" whispered Mac. The man nodded. Mac pointed, and they moved quickly back towards the tree line, through the increasing fog.

"How far?" whispered Ben.

"Half a mile," said Mac, and pulled a radio from his jacket. He turned it on and pressed a button. The radio blinked green once, then no more.

They had gone perhaps two hundred yards when loud voices began behind them.

Mac looked at Ben, who was stumbling now and then. "OK?"

"No food for three days," he said, his voice just a hoarse whisper.

"Me either," said Mac. "Let's go home!"

Mac flipped open the watch cover and checked the compass. He tugged on the other man's sleeve and pulled his path slightly more to the left. "No time to go hide in the woods," he said. "Our guys will be waiting as soon as we can get to them."

Flashlights were visible through the fog behind them, flashlights that were bouncing up and down. Ahead, a blue light appeared in the sky, and the sound of a helicopter.

"We have to win this race," said Mac, no longer trying to be quiet. "As soon as we grab the rope, or whatever they let down, they'll take off again. I don't expect them to land!"

Ben tripped and stumbled to the ground. Mac pulled him up, held his sleeve, and dragged him along. The blue light and the whirring blades were closer. So were the lights behind them. A rifle fired, then there were shouts, and no more shots.

The fog blew apart in front of them, and as a spotlight from above found them, a mesh net fell from the sky. Mac threw Ben onto it, said "Hold on to it!" and shouted up, "Go! Go!" As he grabbed the ropes himself, the net jerked up into the air, and they began swinging and spinning in the air. The helicopter accelerated away, pulling them behind it.

Shots began to fire from behind them, and the red flashes of the gunfire mixed with the white, bouncing lights. A rifle answered from the helicopter. Shells hit the metal of the helicopter, as it flew directly away from the pursuers. The net slowly rose towards the chopper, barely above the trees, and Mac could see the men pulling it up. He looked at the man next to him, and grabbed his arm to keep him close. "Thanks..." came the answer.

Then Ben exclaimed, and groaned. "They hit me," he grunted. "Not bad, just my leg."

They held on for another long minute or two, and then the net was high enough for the men in the helicopter to grab their arms and pull them in. "He's hit," said Mac to the soldier pulling him in. "Get the bleeding stopped."

As they pulled Ben in, another shot from the ground ricocheted from the skin of the chopper and drove into Mac's shoulder. That arm lost all strength, and he barely held on with the other hand. "I'm hit," he gasped, as hands grabbed his coat sleeve and collar. They pulled him up and rolled him onto the floor, and the chopper rolled the other way. He began falling back out, and felt the men holding him as everyone waited for the helicopter to level out again.

"More ground fire," shouted the pilot, and the chopper veered both ways, diving through the sky in random, quick turns. Shells bounced off the hull. Someone clipped a harness on Mac, and he and the man holding him both fell out at the next turn.

The soldier grabbed the net, still hanging below the fuselage, and shouted to Mac, "You OK?"

"Got one arm left. Thanks for the hook!"

They bounced and swung and spun around, dragged through the night sky like a balloon tied to a Roman candle rocket. Mac closed his eyes and waited, hoping not to throw up.

Suddenly the ride settled down.

"We're out, boys!" called the pilot. "Have you down soon."

Other hands pulled the net and the two men into the helicopter, and one of the soldiers knelt down next to Mac. "You took one? Where?"

"Right shoulder, in the back."

His jacket and shirt were quickly stripped back, and someone was probing and squeezing his shoulder.

"You a medic? That hurts worse than the bullet!"

"Nah," the man replied, "but I watched a movie once. Hold still!"

"How's Ben?"

"Seems all right. We got the bleeding stopped, and we'll let the guys on the ground fish the bullet out. Same with you, I guess ... I can't find where it stopped."

"Maybe it went all the way through, like in the Bruce Willis movie..."

"Dream on," said the soldier, pulling Mac's jacket back around him. "Don't you know fiction from reality? This is reality. Want something to eat? Chocolate bar?"

"Yeah," he said, trying to relax. "If this is reality... I think I like the movies better."

And he was asleep before the chocolate bar found him.

# Chapter 2

Mac sat next to his wife's bed, his hand on her shoulder. Her soft breathing made no sound, and the oscilloscopes above all the tubes and wires traced a simple, stable pattern of heartbeats and respiration. He was not comforted.

The new volunteer knocked lightly on the door. He turned.

"Anything I can do for you? I'm Jennie. New on the floor."

"No, Jennie, nothing. Thanks." He turned back to the bed and the displays. Eighty-four percent oxygen, that's low... and staying low. He lifted her hand with the sensor clamped on the first finger, shining its light into the flesh and glowing red.

This may be it. We've all agreed, no more is to be done. But... but... no, if this is her time, I need to just let her go. Let her go, Mac, let her go.

He buried his face in his hands and let the tears come. So many years, so many wonderful memories, and now all he could do was look at her. Look at her, and remember. That soft cheek he had caressed so many times, that mouth he loved to kiss, that mouth with the smile that lit up his life.

The tears flowed.

He must have slept. The sky was almost dark outside the thin curtain over the window, and a tray of food sat untouched on the rolling table to his right. There was another knock on the door.

"Sir?"

He turned, stretching in the chair. "Yes?"

"May I watch her for you, so you can walk a bit, stretch a little?"

He sat back and stared at the ceiling. He looked again at the monitors. Nothing had changed.

"Sure," he said. "Thank you."

He stood and turned, and realized it was the volunteer again. Jennie.

"How long has it been? You must be working a long shift!"

"Covering for a friend. How are you doing? How is your wife?"

He sighed, shook his head, and motioned away the question. He could feel the tears coming again, and he could not speak.

"I'll be here," she said. "Take your time." Gently touching his arm, she nudged him toward the door and took a seat where he had been.

Mac walked aimlessly, and ended up in the cafeteria. He wandered among the people in the lines, found the coffee machines, and drew a large cup of black coffee. He stared at it.

Seems like normally I put something in it ...

But he couldn't remember, so he shook his head and meandered back to the door, out through the lobby, through the main doors, and into the night. The western sky glowed a deep purple, and stars peeked through the city's nighttime glow.

Always there. Constant, never changing. Never hurting, never grieving...

A thin crescent moon appeared between the hotel and the parking garage, as he walked around the hospital. He stared at it.

How do you stay up there? How does a big rock hang there in the sky, spinning around us, never showing its backside, never falling or leaving ...

Another mystery. So many mysteries. How had he met her, and why was she leaving? Part of himself was going away, and there was nothing he could do. Again the tears flowed, and he walked on, barely able to see what was around him. When he finally took a sip of the coffee it was almost cool, and the sky was deep black. The brightest stars fought their way through clouds and reflected neon to reach him, to comfort him, to call him to an eternal perspective.

I know, I know. She's in Your hands. And so am I. Help me, help me.

He stumbled back to the hospital, and the main doors mercifully slid apart to welcome him. The elevator was empty, and the nurse at the main desk on his wife's floor simply nodded to him as he walked by. But there was a kindness in her eyes, a look that must have known the pain and desperate emotions running through a man's soul at such a time.

So many days without her, so many nights in other towns, other countries. Awful places. So many times he left not knowing if he would return, and she was the one who had to endure the waiting, not knowing if he were alive... or even if she would ever know what had happened to him. But each time he had returned — mostly in one piece — and they had resumed their life together. Until the next time he left.

And now she was at peace, he hoped, and she was the one leaving, and he knew she would not return.

How would he live?

He could not think about it. Beyond her there was nothing, just an empty, dark place in his mind. Nothing worth doing, nowhere worth going.

He realized he was standing at her door, and the light had been dimmed. The volunteer was still there, sitting in his chair, holding his wife's hand. Praying? Maybe. He couldn't tell. He stood there watching for a while, and eventually the volunteer sat back in the chair and he tapped on the door.

"Oh, it's you. Please come in." She quickly got up. 'Jennie,' that's what her name tag said. He remembered.

"She's still sleeping, as peaceful as before. The O2 is a bit lower, though."

He looked at the displays, and nodded. "Thank you."

She slipped out and he settled into the chair. Suddenly it was morning, and the room was bright.

The doctor came about ten, and checked her over. He sat down on the little rolling stool and turned to Mac.

"I think we're close. Her oxygen is failing, and given the way the cancer has progressed, anything we do to stop it would just make her remaining time miserable."

Mac nodded. This was not a new conversation.

"She may not last the day. How are you doing?"

Mac shook his head, and did not trust himself to speak.

"You've met with the case manager, and have all your arrangements in place, I understand."

Yes, he did.

"Call me, or have the nurses do it, if you need me."

OK. He nodded.

The doctor stood to leave, squeezed his shoulder, and was gone.

At noon there was a tapping, and the volunteer — Jennie — was there with the food tray. Mac was eager to talk with someone, to divert his mind, and asked her if she could stay a few minutes.

"Certainly. I'm Jennie, but you know that," she said, looking self-consciously at her name tag. "You are ... Mac?"

"Yes. Tell me, Jennie, what do you do when you're not consoling old men at the hospital?"

She smiled. "Haven't consoled any lately, now that you mention it. But — I'm a journalist. And I teach, at the university in town."

"Care and compassion?"

"No," she laughed, and he relaxed a bit. There was something healing in that laugh. "Just journalism."

"And what do you journal about, when you can do whatever you want? Do you write about food, or travel... or the labyrinth of deep human emotions people experience in hospitals?"

"I'm sorry. I know this is a tough, tough time. Umm ... mainly about people, I guess, and sometimes about how we work our way through the difficulties we face. I'm not much on cooking, or sewing, or decorating.. or whatever's popular ... I was a dancer, and I like some sports, so those show up in my writing too."

"Sports? Like what?"

"I love racquetball. And dance ... that's kind of a sport, I guess. Volleyball, skeet, ..."

"Skeet? You shoot?"

"A bit. Went to state, did OK. And I'm fair with a pistol. How about you? What do you do to earn a living?"

He looked down for a moment. "Mostly things I can't talk about... but I guess I'm fair with a pistol, too. No good at all on a dance floor, though!"

"Pool?"

"Billiards? You know what a cue stick is for?"

She laughed. "Most girls don't, I suppose. But I grew up with brothers, and it was self-defense! That and ping-pong!"

"Yeah, sounds like my family..."

He looked back at his wife, breathing softly. Oxygen at 80, and slowly dropping.

"I need to go. Bless you." She stood and turned to leave.

"Thanks," he said. "Thank you. You've been very helpful."

She nodded, and disappeared.

# Chapter 3

Mac stood on the back deck, staring at the zinnias and snapdragons, the rose bushes and the carefully-tended bed of day lilies.

He took a long, slow drink of the iced tea in his hand, and sank into the plastic Adirondack lawn chair. The one with the empty chair next to it.

She really is gone. So this is what it feels like.

Not a good feeling.

Why did I spend so much time away from her?

"You were doing good things," a voice chided him from the back of his mind. "People needed you, you saved lives, you protected people, you may have kept a whole country from falling into hardcore tyranny — at least for another decade or two."

That's what his mind said.

That's not what his heart said.

His heart said, "Shut up."

An hour later he realized the sun had gone down, the mosquitos were devouring his bare ankles, and the iced tea was no longer even ice, much less iced tea.

He lifted himself up and dragged into the house. The dark house. He turned on the living room lights as he came through the door, and listened.

Nothing. She would have had the Beethoven channel from Pandora playing by now, to carry them into the evening hours.

"I should do something about dinner," said his mind. "Why?" responded his heart.

I need to go somewhere, do something.

He bought a ticket an hour later. Then he canceled it.

The next morning, with a small overnight bag and a few essentials, he backed out of the garage and pushed the "close the door" button on the remote. Somehow the closing of the door felt like the closing of an era, and he drove away not quite as sad as he had been for ... a month? Two months? Too long.

He stopped at the post office and asked them to hold mail until further notice. How long? Not sure, he told them. Not at all sure.

The leaves were starting to turn in New England. Good time to go wander. Maybe a good time to buy a decent camera, and quit depending on a phone. Get something with a zoom lens, and something that doesn't need film.

He drove north, staying away from the big cities and taking side roads wherever they looked interesting.

At a camera store in a small town outside of Boston he bought a used Canon Rebel XT and a small zoom lens.

Not too heavy. Nice. And not too expensive, so if I lose it, not a big deal.

As he walked out of the camera store, he started seeing pictures. The intersection, with the American flag over the hardware store, and the older fellow with a cane just entering the street to cross. Sunlight coming from behind those buildings, backlighting the man's white hair.

Twenty pictures later, he looked around to remember where he had parked. Had he eaten breakfast?

Couldn't remember.

"Is this what life is like, now that she's gone?" he wondered. Forgetting things, no goals, no direction? His stomach voted, and he decided the Cozy Cafe looked just fine, and it probably wasn't too late for breakfast.

"Howdy, ma'am," he said, taking off his hat and slipping into a booth. The waitress stopped placing silverware and a menu in front of him, and said, "Excuse me?"

"Good morning."

"That's what I thought you said. Good morning. Coffee?"

"Sure. And some Splenda?"

She paused again, and asked, "Sugar OK? Or the pink stuff, the saccharin?"

"No Splenda? Equal?"

"Equal to ... what?"

"Sugar will be great, and some ... some milk for it, please."

"Be right back."

Maybe I'm a little too far off the main roads, he thought. Actually I'm not too sure where I am.

He pulled out the iPhone, opened up the map app, and touched the arrow that centers the display on wherever you are.

Amazing, he thought. And I thought it was a phone. It's a computer, and they added a phone thing so people would buy it!

"What else can I bring you?" asked the waitress.

"A life?"

She set the coffee down, and pulled two Splenda packs from her apron. "Found some. Just for you. So, what's got you down?"

He leaned back and really looked at her for the first time. She honestly cared, and it showed in her eyes.

"Thank you," he said. "Just lost my wife, and I'm having trouble adjusting."

She nodded, and set an open menu in front of him. "This one's on me. Order everything you like, and don't worry about eating it all. Seriously. Have a wonderful breakfast. The cook is good."

She touched his shoulder briefly as she turned away to seat another customer.

After the oatmeal, the fried eggs, the bacon, the eggs benedict, the stack of toast, the sausage, and the fresh fruit, he decided a stack of three pancakes would be perfect. And some hot chocolate, and yes, he would like whipped cream on it, thanks.

She brought the ticket when he pushed the last plate away and felt like he would never be able to eat again. The amount due showed "$0.00", and was signed with a smiley face.

"Are you a church-going girl, may I ask?"

"Sure am."

"Say a prayer for me now and then, if you would. I'll get through this, but I sure would like some help now and then."

"You got it. So, I gather you're passing through? Looking at the trees?"

"I would like to, if I can make it back to my truck!"

She laughed. "Glad you liked the food. Listen, turn left on the state road at the next light, and follow that road for about a hundred miles. You'll like what you see."

"Excellent," he said. "You've been most kind."

He slipped out while she was waiting on another customer at the other end of the cafe, and left fifty dollars under the ticket. A tip, he thought, just a tip. And well-earned.

The state road led quickly out of town and into wooded country, spread with farms and scattered homes. The maples and beeches were in full color, and every now and then a Bradford pear did its best to compete. Finding places to pull off the road to grab the pictures was the hardest part of the day.

As he sipped coffee at a Love's truck stop that evening, the phone rang.

"Mac, how are you doing? Haven't heard from you since she's been gone."

"It's tough, boss. I'm wandering New England at the moment, to get my mind out of neutral, and my body out of the house."

"How about a bodyguard role for a few days?"

"Not sure I can stay that focused, truthfully. If you've got a job watching paint dry, maybe I could handle that."

"All right, I'll bring in someone else. Stay in touch, would you?"

"Sure. I will."

He watched the sun set behind the 18-wheelers and gas pumps. Romantic, he thought. What am I doing?

# Chapter 4

Fifty miles further down the road, it occurred to him that he was low on gas and had no plans for where to stay that evening. He pulled into a faded gas station in the next village, wondering if it was even open. The paint looked like it must have been an Exxon at one time. A neon sign flickered in the window, and the lights over the two pumps were mostly on.

He opened the gas cap and inserted the pump, and just as he set the handle to stay on something stuck him in the ribs and a voice said, "Got any cash?"

Without really thinking about it, he pivoted, twisted the gun out of the man's hand, and pinned his face against the glass of the gas pump. He kicked the gun up against the back tire, and then began wondering what his next move would be.

"No, actually, I don't have any to spare. How about you?"

"I'm ... no, I'm broke. What do you think?"

"Doing drugs, or just liquor?"

"Had a hamburger in mind, actually. Do you have to smash my face into the glass like this?"

"I could put it on the driveway, if you'd rather."

"No," the choked voice said from just above the meter ticking away the gallons. "This is fine."

"What am I going to do with you, that's really the question. Any police in this town?"

"My cousin."

"Sweet. Nice for you, not so nice for everyone else."

"Look, I'm sorry, can I go?"

"No, I don't think so. I need to buy you a hamburger."

"What?"

"They sell food here?"

"Yeah, sandwiches and stuff."

'Would that work for you?"

"You serious? Anything would work, I'm starving."

"All right, drop your wallet on the ground, and then walk halfway to the store. Stand there. When I'm done pumping gas, I'll follow you and buy you something, and maybe give your license back. A man shouldn't have to go to jail for armed robbery just to get a meal."

"What are you going to do with my gun?"

"You'll never see it again. Too much of a temptation, best I can tell."

They sat at a table with small benches in the back of a shabby cafe at the gas station. The young man was obviously nervous.

"What are you doing, holding people up? You're not very good at it, and you'll get hurt. Never mind arrested!"

The only answer was a hung head and a finger tracing a pattern on the worn Formica table top.

"What's your name? Maybe we can start there. Oh, never mind, I've got your ID... Thomas? Tom?"

"Yes, sir."

"Been in the military?"

"Yes, sir. Did a tour in Afghanistan, and got out, but there's no jobs here at home. I'm about to be on the street."

"Well, a jail cell is a place to sleep, but I can't recommend it from what I've seen. Sure you want to go there?"

"No, sir, I don't."

Tom leaned back in the bench. "Why are you being so nice to me?"

"Hate to see a wasted life," said Mac, "and you're about to waste yours."

Tom nodded. "Got any advice?"

"What are you good at?"

"Hunting terrorists in the desert."

"You should be better at hand to hand combat, then."

"Wasn't expecting you to react like that. Over there, you expected it all the time."

"And I expect you've gotten rusty. How long you been out?"

"Six months."

Mac nodded. "No work?"

"Nothing. With that new insurance law, all the jobs went to part time, and businesses were already not hiring ... you probably know why."

"Yeah, until everyone knows which way to jump, they hunker down. Just makes sense."

"Yeah, that's what it is. But in your day, didn't we fight a war against these same ideas?"

"In my day? Do I look that old? I know I'm not taking care of myself but ... really?"

"Sorry, sir. No, you don't."

Hamburgers finally came, and Tom devoured his before the waitress had made it back to the counter.

"Here," said Mac. "Take this one too. I just ate, an hour ago."

"Thank you, sir, if you mean it."

Mac watched the second hamburger disappear, along with a big coffee.

"OK, I believe you. Here's your wallet back."

"Thank you, sir."

"But really... what are you good at? How are you going to earn a living?"

"Went to the army from high school, so ... don't really know. Shop class was great, and drafting, and such. Didn't do so well with English, and biology, and all that."

"But you got the degree? And you know how to use a bandsaw, a lathe, drill press, all that?"

"Yes, sir, and I got good grades, mostly."

"Willing to move?"

"Yes, sir, anywhere."

Mac looked at his watch. "It's not too late in Phoenix. Hold on." He pulled out his cell phone, flipped through the names, and touched one.

"Mac here. Is this Kendrick? Hey, my friend, how are you?" He set the phone down on the table and put it on speaker.

"Great, Mac, what's up? Don't hear from you often, and never at night!"

"Can I call in a favor?"

"Anything, any time, no questions asked."

"I'm in a diner somewhere in New England with a young man who needs a job. Back from Afghanistan, did well in high school shop, and needs a step onto the ladder of success. Can you put him to work?"

"As soon as he gets here. We just captured a big project, and I've got people who can train him as they go. How soon can he be here?"

"Just a minute." He put the phone on mute.

"How soon can you be in Phoenix?"

"I have a car, sir, but no money for gas."

Mac took the phone off mute. "Give him three days to make the drive. Text me the address where he should report to work on ... let's see ... Wednesday morning."

"Will do, chief. If he doesn't work out, can I fire him?"

"Of course. But I think he just needs a chance."

"Done. Thanks. Saves me one more fee to the recruiters!"

Mac wrote out the address on a napkin and handed it to Tom. "Get me a US map from the rack over there, would you?"

When Tom returned, Mac spread out the map. Dividing the distance into approximately thirds, he traced a route. "I'm thinking you can get to St. Louis by tomorrow night... you'll need a little time to pack and throw some stuff away, and turn in the keys. You're renting?"

"Yes, sir."

"Then maybe Oklahoma City the next night? Hmm. Probably better to push on to, oh, maybe Amarillo the next night, and make the third day's drive shorter, on into Phoenix. Hold on."

He dialed the phone again. "Yes, my member number? Here it is. Need some reservations using points: tomorrow night in St. Louis, the next night in Amarillo, and then three nights in Phoenix near ... let me see ... oh, actually in Glendale. Just book for one adult, whatever brand is available that uses the least points, and email me the reservations. Oh, and also email the reservations to ...."

"What's your email address?" Tom wrote it on the napkin and turned it for Mac to read. "That's an odd one!" He turned his attention back to the phone.

"Here's the email address ... and the person checking in will be ... Tom Simmons, in all locations."

"No, that's all. Thanks. Oh, wait — make it five nights in Glendale. Got it? Thanks."

He disconnected the phone call, and looked at Tom for a moment. "I'm not wasting my time, am I?"

"No, sir, not at all! Thank you, sir!"

"I figure Kendrick will work you so hard you'll be too exhausted the first night, and it will take you a couple of days to get an apartment. So ... how much cash are you going to need? Gas for the trip, food for three days ... really, a week ... got clothes good enough to work in?"

They settled on a number, and Mac pulled several twenty dollar bills from his wallet. "If you don't show up out there, I'll file charges for robbery ... armed robbery, as I recall, so that's a felony ... and give them your ID info."

He lifted his phone, pointed the camera at Tom, and pressed the button. "And your picture, of course!"

Tom laughed.

"You look relaxed. The idea of my filing charges is pleasant to hear?"

"No, sir, and you won't need to do that. I'm just amazed at what you're doing, and so glad to have a way out of this hole!"

Tom leaned forward. "What do you do? Why are you here?"

Now it was Mac's turn to draw patterns on the table. "Personal protection. Undercover stuff. Did some time in Iran, Turkey, Egypt, even some interesting places now and then. Not sure why I'm here, except to meet you ... obviously ... so now you owe me one. Here's an email address you can use ..."

He wrote on another napkin.

"I want to know how to reach you, and that you're succeeding. You promised."

"In case you need to call in a favor sometime?"

"Exactly."

"And maybe to repay the loan?"

"That would be appreciated as well."

"So what was the favor, with Mr. Kendrick, if I may ask?"

Mac rubbed his eyes. "It's getting late, isn't it?"

As he stood up, he added, "Pulled him out of a firefight in Iraq, full of holes. He would've done the same for me."

They walked out into the cool night air.

"Do good, you hear?"

"Yes, sir," said Tom, and saluted as well as any vet could. "I'll make you proud."

Mac returned the salute and watched Tom disappear down the street.

"Now where am I going?"

He climbed into his truck, and pulled out onto the little road.

"I think I'll go home."

# Chapter 5

Three days later, he woke up in his own bed with a bright sun in the window shades and a face in great need of a shave. A shower would be a good idea, too!

After cleaning up and scrounging for some breakfast, he looked out the back window. That yard man had not come.

Wait, he thought. I'm the yard man. Where have I been?

Feeling sorry for myself. Time to shake that off. Wonder if I've got any gas in the mower?

Whacking weeds and roaring around the yard on a pretend tractor helped for a while, but by lunchtime he was feeling lonely again. She wasn't there to throw a sandwich together and offer a thank-you kiss.

Would not be there, ever.

By dinner time he was out on the streets again, just looking for somewhere else to be.

This is ridiculous, he thought. I need someone. Need to be with people, making friends, doing things with people.

But who? No one wanted to hear what he did for a living, what he had done over the years. It wasn't pretty.

"If I ever marry again, I won't spend so much time away," he promised himself. "Life is too short. Way too short."

It was more than a year later when Jennie arrived at the hospital to start her shift in the candy-striped apron of the volunteer team and found a note waiting.

"Jennie, whose last name I don't know, this is Mac. You were very kind to me as my wife was dying — 18 months ago, now — I was just thinking about that time, and I wondered if I could take you to dinner and express my thanks."

A phone number was the only signature.

Yes, she decided. Yes, you can. I enjoyed those few minutes.

He picked her up at the hospital door a week later, and held the door for her.

"I haven't asked you what you would like to do for dinner," he admitted. "I suppose I should ask now, so I know which way to point the truck!"

"How about Italian?" she offered. "Haven't done that for a while, and those tend to be quieter than the steak houses!"

"Good," he said. "Suits me fine."

They pulled into Giovanni's parking lot a few minutes later. She started to get out, and he touched her arm.

"Just a minute, young lady. You may have forgotten your manners, but I remember mine!" He came around and opened the door. "If you please?"

The restaurant was as quiet as she had hoped, and their only company was the candle centering their table. She buttered a slice of the almost-too-hot garlic bread after the waitress took their orders.

"Ooh, this looks wonderful!"

"So do you," he said. "May I be so forward as to ask if you are ... involved with anyone? I don't want to be intruding on another relationship!"

"My," she said, "aren't you forward!"

"Well ... I tend to be direct. Everything on the table, so to speak. And I've learned recently ... you were there! ... how little time we really have on this earth. I guess I'm less inclined to let it go by ..."

"Wasted?"

"Yeah, something like that."

He was quiet, and Jennie decided he was waiting for an answer.

"I'm not seeing anyone, as a matter of fact. I think I intimidate them!"

He laughed. "Well, better for me, then! How do you intimidate them?"

"Most men are a little taken aback by losing at every sport they suggest ... and then, when they realize I have a concealed carry permit, well ... you can imagine!"

He laughed again, and visibly relaxed.

"Jennie," he said, leaning forward on his elbows, "I like you. If it suits you — and please let me know if it doesn't — I'd like to spend some regular time together, and see if we might be a match. But you know nothing about me, so I should offer a little background."

"You are the most forward man I've ever met," she smiled. "But I like that... and really, I know a lot about you. I knew you in one of the hardest times of your life, and I watched you then. Remember, I'm a journalist. I've learned to see a lot through small windows that are open for a short time!"

Her lasagna arrived, and his veal parmigiana as well.

"May I offer a blessing?" he asked.

"Please."

They bowed their heads, and he said, "Thank you, Father, for everything. Your will be done."

She looked up. "That was it?"

He smiled. "Really, at the end of the day... what else is there to say?"

"You said you couldn't talk about your work," she remembered as she sliced into the layers of cheese and pasta, "but is there anything I really should know about it?"

"I protect people," he said. "All types, all over the world. Been beat up by the best, and have tried to return the favor... and live to tell about it."

"So you could teach me some things."

He paused and studied her.

"As I recall, you've already learned some of them! But, sure ... depending on what you want to know! Grammar and syntax are some of my worst enemies — you're on your own there!"

"Got those covered."

The waitress refreshed their iced tea, and he asked for coffee.

"Dessert?"

"Well ... since you asked ... crème brûlée?"

"Do you have spumoni?" she added.

"Ahh," he said, "I can tell you know your way around an Italian menu! Traveled much?"

"Yes, unfortunately I know my way around too many airports!"

"Me, too."

"Anything else I should know about you?"

He thought about it for a minute, sipping the hot coffee.

"Well, here's a random thought. I've spent my life being gone, being away from the one I love. I don't want to do that anymore. But what I do is all I know ... so, would you come with me? Could we work together? I could train you..."

"I'd love it!" she said. "I would absolutely love it! But wait ... I hardly know you ... was that a proposal?"

He sat back, staring at her. "I think maybe it was... yes, I think it was. Jennie, whose last name I still don't know, will you marry me, Mac whose last name you still don't know?"

"Oh, my goodness. What a first date! Tell you what ... let me go powder my nose and think about this!"

She wandered off to find the restrooms.

Actually, she liked the idea very much. Nothing else was on the horizon, she was aching for some excitement, and along comes ... this. Were there any warning signs? Was this man reliable?

She returned to the table as the waitress refilled his coffee. He looked up, and interrupted what she was about to say. "Jennie, I'm fifty. I think you're much younger than that. If that's any concern at all to you, then let's not even continue the conversation ..."

She held up a hand. "Mr. Anonymous, I could care less. And you're probably way off on how young you think I am!"

"Don't care," he said. "Absolutely don't care."

"Well, we're even then. So tell me straight out: are you reliable? If I placed my life in your hands, would I regret it?"

He stood up, knelt down beside her chair, and said, "Miss Jennie Whatever-Your-Name-Is, I want to marry you, and you will never, ever, ever regret it. I promise."

She smiled, and looked into the most genuine eyes she had ever seen.

"Well, in that case, I'll have to think about it."

She laughed at his expression. "OK, I've thought about it. Yes, Mr. Whoever-You-Are, I will marry you."

# Chapter 6

"Honey, I'm gonna do something crazy."

"What, again?" Mac looked up from the review of the new Glock .380.

"I'm going to write a novel."

"Yeah? That is crazy. What else?"

"I'm going to get some friends to do it with me."

"So you each write half? You write the funny stuff, they write the boring stuff? Or you write every other chapter ... paragraph? ... I've got it, you write every other sentence! Only a journalist could do something like this!"

She waited.

"OK," he said. "How does that work?"

"We each do our own, silly. Our own novel. But the trick is to do it fast, so you have to let the creative side of you take over. So fast there's no time to carefully plan and edit and adjust, you just have to go!"

He stared at her. "How fast?"

"Fifty thousand words in a month. Thirty days."

"Umm..." He looked around. How much is that, really? He found a paperback. "Is this fifty thousand words?" He tossed it to her.

She flipped through it. "More like ninety, I would think."

"So half that, in a month?"

"Yeah. The idea is that you can do things with a deadline that you'll never get around to doing otherwise."

"Well. How many friends were you thinking of losing, with this approach?"

"All of them, I suspect!"

"Really. How many? Who?"

"Three or four of us, I think. So we could sit around the same table now and then and write together."

"But each doing your own thing."

"Yeah. Totally different, I would guess."

"But you'd each want your own music, right? So you'd need headphones. You'll be writing a Kung Fu battle, listening to some hot lead guitar work, and your friend will want Vivaldi for her nothing-ever-happens Victorian romance."

"Earbuds, silly. No problem."

He nodded. "Got some people in mind?"

"No ... but I'm thinking about it."

"So, I'm on my own for dinner for ... how long? A month?"

"Actually, I'll need you to cook for me too!" He grimaced, and she laughed. "Someone's got to cook while I write!"

"You've had my cooking, right?"

"Yes, and you're great with steaks, desserts, certain potato dishes ... not so much on vegetables, salads, or anything generally considered healthy!"

"I'm liking this." He smiled, thinking of the possibilities. "Driver's choice, you know. So we get to eat whatever I want to fix, for ... a month?"

She grimaced. "Umm ... can we negotiate?"

"When do we start?" he said, rubbing his hands together. "I'll need to get a new grill, and stock up on some ... let's see, you're more for Chardonnay, aren't you?"

"Boy, that'll help my prose!"

"But the goal is to write fast, you said. So, uninhibited. Emotionally driven, not mentally planning and structuring things. Yes, I think Chardonnay, some Zinfandel, I'll work on the list. When do we start?"

She laughed. "So much for selling you on the idea! The problem will be if I decide NOT to do it!"

"You know," he said, after they sat silent for a moment, "this needs to be fiction, right?"

"Sure. No time to research."

"So, you've got a problem."

"OK?"

"Look at my life. Look at yours."

"Yes..."

"What's left? Any fiction you can make up will be something I've already done, or you've already reported!"

She laughed. "I'll just need to be a bit more creative. Think of some ... boring adventures, lame crises, ordinary disasters ... so there won't be any overlap with the real thing."

"There you go. Perfect. And start soon, so the real thing doesn't come along and pre-empt your novel!"

"This is really good," she said, scooping another spoonful of ice cream and mixing it in with the fudge and peanuts.

"Dairy Queen isn't the only place that knows how to do that," laughed Mac, stuffing the carton of Blue Bell Homemade Vanilla back into the freezer. "So how's your book going?"

"It's only day three... I've got the whole month."

"So you're behind schedule already?"

"This is really good," she said, getting the ice cream back out.

"Changing the subject?"

"Of course! I'm no fool. Besides, I'm doing pretty well for someone who has no idea what she's writing about!"

"You're writing a novel ... fifty thousand words in 30 days ..."

"Thirty one. That's one reason I'm doing it in July!"

"OK, smart. So thirty-one days... that's seventeen hundred and something words per day, right?"

She nodded.

"So I should stock up on Blue Bell, right?"

"Right!"

"Still got time for your day job?"

"I'm a teacher, remember? This is July."

"Oh. Of course. Got it. More ice cream?"

Silence.

"Umm... be quiet, because you're writing?"

She blew him a kiss, and went back to staring at the notebook screen, fingers running silently across the backlit keys.

Mac wandered back into the kitchen and punched the power button on the water kettle. His phone jingled.

"Yes?"

A few minutes later Jennie came into the kitchen and sat down next to him.

"Who was it? You never spoke."

"Didn't say. Told me I needed to enjoy the next four days, because they would be my last."

"How generous. Four days. Think he's taking a slow bus to get here?"

He smiled. "I'm trying to remember the voice ... seems like I must know him, or why would he bother?"

"Any idea?"

"No ... a lot of possibilities."

She put her hands over his, folded in front of him.

"I can't believe that. I've been married to you, what, a year now? And I can't think of more than ... a dozen? ... guys that would like to see you put away!"

He smiled at her. "The list is actually a bit longer."

After a pause, he added, "The question is, do they know me well enough to get the job done?"

Jennie went to the sink and poured a glass of water. "Did you want to make tea, or something? The water's hot."

"Chai, please. The red bag by the cup."

She stirred in some Splenda and brought it to him. "What do we do?"

"First, let's give him a name. What do you like?"

"Well, I'm a writer ..." she stretched ... "but it's late, and I need another four hundred words tonight, so I don't want to waste a lot of time on him. How about ... Goofy? Dopey? There's got to be a good name there, somewhere..."

"Ratface," said Mac. "That'll do. Now go back to your story, and let me think about ... Ratface ... and how we'll deal with him."

She made the four hundred words before his tea needed refilling, and came back to the kitchen. Coming up behind him, she wrapped her arms around him and kissed the top of his head. He took her hand and drew her around to the other chair.

"Let's take a road trip," he said. "See who follows."

"I like it," she said. "I'll write, you duck, and we'll see the country while he chases us."

# Chapter 7

Jimmy leaned way back in the reclining desk chair and tried again to blow a smoke ring.

"Must need a different pipe. That's gotta be it."

Snap scowled. "Ain't the pipe, boss. It ain't the pipe that's blowing the smoke up there. You gotta do somethin' different with your mouth, or somethin'. I seen people do it, but ... "

Jimmy took a deep breath through the pipe, and the tobacco coals in the basin burned bright. He made his mouth into the best circle he could, and softly blew towards the ceiling. The smoke drifted out in a long, straight line, and fell apart in the breeze of the fan.

"It's the fan! Can't do it with the fan going!"

"You're right, boss. Should'a thought of that myself. The fan is the problem."

Snap walked to the window and stared out into the blackness. Deserted factory, abandoned buildings, no lights.

"So, what about your other problem? You gave him four days."

"Yeah, so tomorrow is day one. What's the question?"

"You sending me to finish it, right? Ain't said so, but that's the way it always works, kinda."

"Yeah, Snap, I was going to talk to you about that. Would you be available to take out someone for me? Someone giving me a little heartburn just by being alive?"

"We're talkin' Mac, right? The Mac I know?"

"Yes, Snap, I believe you are acquainted with the gentleman. Might even have a few reminders of when you last met."

Snap rubbed his hand across the ragged scar under his beard. "Yeah, boss, I might."

"So, what are you thinking?"

"You care how I do it?"

"Messy and painful, would be my preference. And that woman of his, she's about as bad."

"He's got a woman now?"

"Yeah, a teacher. Younger than him."

"Well, she can watch, then I'll get rid of her too. No good leaving witnesses around."

"He's all yours. Ten grand for him, maybe five for her, just for the trouble?"

"Yeah, boss, that's fine. Couple dollars for the shells, and a few bucks for gas, 'bout all it's gonna cost me, so ... yeah, that's fine. When?"

"When we spoke ... actually, I don't remember him saying anything, but nonetheless, when we spoke, I told him he had four days. So, tomorrow is Monday ... do it on Friday. We'll give him that long to wish he'd never stuck his stupid nose into our operation."

"Where is the 'gentleman' now?"

"Here's the address." Jimmy tore off a piece of printer paper and scribbled it down. "But I have no idea where he'll be on Friday. You'll have to find that out, but when we spoke a few minutes ago, he was home."

Snap looked at the paper. "'Not all that far from here ... he might skedaddle, if he thinks you're serious."

Snap glanced at Jimmy. "Does he think you're serious?"

Jimmy smiled and nodded. "No doubt about it."

"Then I'll probably head over there first thing in the morning, and not let him sneak away. Can I use my favorite ride?"

"It's all yours, my friend. And thank you."

As Snap turned to the door, Jimmy added, "By the way ... did you ever tell me where the name 'Snap' came from?"

Snap paused, and without looking back said, "You know what they say, boss ... I could tell you, but then I'd have to kill you." And he walked out.

# Chapter 8

"How are you set for ammunition?"

"I'm good," she said. "The .380 slips into my purse just fine, and I have enough cartridges for anything I might need to do. How about you?"

Long before dawn the garage door closed behind them and the black F150 pulled away into the fog drifting over the neighborhood from the wetlands that wrapped around the subdivision.

"Drive south, if it doesn't matter," said Jennie. "So the sun won't be on my screen!" After an hour, she looked up from her laptop. "See anyone following us?"

"No," said Mac, quietly, "but this is day one. My guess is that we'll see him when we stop for dinner tomorrow, and then again at lunch the next day."

"No matter where we are?"

"No matter."

"He sounded good?"

"Yeah, I think this one is pretty good, or he wouldn't have played this game. Which narrows it down a bit. I'm going to guess who it is before it's over."

Mac was quiet for a moment, then asked, "By the way, did you notice the black car we passed, just after leaving the neighborhood?"

"I did," said Jennie. "A small one, sporty?"

Mac nodded. "Porsche Carrera. Expensive. Beautiful. Don't remember the last time I saw one. If you ever want to get me a really nice Christmas gift ... red would be great ..."

She laughed. "In the meantime, want to stop in at a range somewhere along our path and practice a little?"

"Sure. That'll give him something to think about."

When they stopped for lunch the sign in a white cinder block building offered the clue: "CHL/LTC classes here."

They rented eye protection and ear muffs at the counter, signed papers that assured everyone the range was not at fault for anything bad that might happen, bought two boxes of shells and found an open lane.

As they paid the bill, Mac asked the clerk about the holster he was wearing.

"Crossbreed. Love 'em. Name's Chuck, by the way."

"Thanks," said Mac. "By the way, we're being followed. Threatened. If someone comes through and asks about us, describes us, would you mind letting us know?" He handed Chuck a card that simply said "Mac" and the phone number.

The clerk raised an eyebrow and looked at him quizzically. "Kind of an unusual business card," he said.

"Personal protection," Mac smiled. "Less is more."

Chuck laughed. He looked at Jennie. "Is he on the level?"

"He's the best," Jennie assured him.

He nodded. "You got it. Take care."

They walked to a sandwich shop in the next block for lunch. Mac tipped his hat to the lady who met them at the door.

"What's the best seat in the house?" he asked.

She led the way to a booth at the end of the aisle. "Great view of people passing by, and close to the kitchen so it's easy to keep your coffee hot."

Jennie squeezed her arm as they took their seats. "Thank you.

You're good with people. How long have you been here?"

"In the town? Or in this diner?"

"I'm guessing at least twenty years in the diner," said Jennie. "As we walked through, it seemed to me that everyone in the place knew you."

"Pretty close," said the waitress. "Belle is the name, by the way. Yours?"

"Mac," he said, touching the brim of his hat, "and my sweetheart Jennie."

"What can I get for you?"

"What's best?"

"It's a German place, mainly, so the sausage is excellent, and if you like a Reuben..."

The sandwiches arrived quickly and hot, with plenty of napkins. As Mac took the second bite from his Reuben, he paused. Jennie cocked her head, the question on her face. He nodded, and went on with the sandwich.

"I think that was him," he said when he could get the words out. "Not anyone I recognize, but I would know that walk, that look, that expression, in 20 different countries!"

"Description?"

"Black pants, dark blue Polo shirt, too big and too long ..."

"Hiding firearms?"

"Absolutely. Black beard, starting to bald, completely unfriendly ..."

"Why do you think it was him?"

"He was looking for someone, but not to say hello. And from the way he looked around, he had never been here before. I think he saw my truck at the range, knows we're not there, and is looking for us."

Mac pulled out his phone, and nodded. "Got a message from our friend at the range. 'He came asking about you. Five foot nine, black beard. Told him nothing. Be careful.'"

As she put their ticket on the table, Belle said, "You're not from here. What brings you to town?"

Jennie glanced at Mac before answering. "Someone's following us," she said. "Threatening us. So we thought we'd ... take a drive."

Belle nodded. "And a window to watch people go by is a good thing, right?"

Mac laughed. "You're good! May I ask a favor?"

"Whatever you like," said Belle, "but if it's on the menu I have to charge for it!"

"No, just a favor ... on the outside chance that whoever is after us comes along behind us and asks questions, would you let us know?"

"Sure. Just give me a phone number to go with 'Mac and Jennie,' and I'll be glad to."

Mac laid another card on the table. Belle picked it up, turned it over, and back over.

"Well," she said. "Short and sweet. If they come asking, I'll pass the word."

"You're a dear," said Jennie. "Mac, do something interesting for a tip."

"Absolutely," he smiled, and added another zero to the number on the credit card slip.

At the door, he motioned for Jennie to stay inside as he stepped out onto the sidewalk. He stretched, casually looking around, then wandered down the sidewalk. When he was almost a block away, Jennie came out, crossed the street in a brisk walk, and headed the same direction on the other side of the street.

Mac crossed over the street, slipped into the driver's seat, and eased down low enough that no one looking from behind would see anyone on the driver's side. Jennie went into the range briefly, then came out and got in on the other side.

After a few minutes, Mac started it and immediately pulled out into traffic. He turned right at the first corner, turned right again, pulled up to the curb and stopped.

"Stay low," he said. After half a minute, a black car came around the corner a bit too fast. "Looking for us," he commented, as it accelerated past. "Let's wait."

In about five minutes the car came back the other direction, and Jennie wrote down the license plate.

"That's not from here," she exclaimed. "Could be a rental car, but I've never seen them rent those. Surely they have some, but ..."

"No, it's an out-of-state license that's had a little too much wear and tear for Avis. Someone drove it here. From where? Jersey? New York State?"

"Did not recognize it. Good homework assignment, huh? Learn the plates?"

"An excellent assignment. But did anything else strike you about that car?"

"Small, black, sporty ... "

She looked at him. "Porsche Carrera?"

"Exactly. Shall we go?"

Jennie pulled up the mapping app. "There's a county road number on the cross-street at the next corner... how about if we take a drive in the country?"

"Any idea where it goes?" asked Mac as he pulled into the street and paused at the corner.

"Away from the main highway."

"I like it," he said, and turned left, driving away from town and past some frame houses with pier-and-beam supports under the wooden porches. "Looks like these were built early last century ... used to live in one like that. Did you know the wiring in the walls of those houses does not even have insulation?"

"What?"

"Really. It's called 'knob and tube,' and the wires are run between ceramic conductors. If you open the wall to do anything to it, you have to replace all of it ... codes don't allow it to stay."

"I guess not. Sounds dangerous."

"The one I grew up in, the whole house ran on extension cords!"

"You had electricity when you grew up?"

"If only I had a pillow to throw at you..."

"Maybe we'll find a hotel tonight that has one."

"Speaking of that ... where are we going, exactly?"

She shrugged. "Away from Blackbeard, that's all I know."

"Blackbeard? That works. Probably a better name for him, although I was getting fond of Ratface."

After a few minutes, he added thoughtfully, "You know, Ratface is not the one who called me."

"Really! How do you know?"

"The voice on the phone was refined. Polite. Evil, but polished. The guy who walked past, Ratface, probably can't even spell his own name. A hired gun."

The frame houses were replaced by corn fields, and here and there a field that looked freshly mown down, almost to raw dirt. The afternoon sun drifted down.

"Think he's followed us?"

"Haven't noticed anyone," Mac said, peering at the rear view mirror. "But I hadn't noticed him before we had lunch, either. He'll find us."

"What do we do then?"

"Play cat and mouse until Friday, I suppose ... but you know, he's not the problem. Not the real problem."

She nodded. "I think I'll put him in my story. We'll know him better in a couple of days, right?"

"Oh, yeah. And he'll know us better, too!"

Jennie touched her iPhone. After a minute she looked up. "In about a mile, there's a country road — can't read the number — that goes off to the right. In about five miles, it would put us on the Interstate."

"You'd like a hotel with two pillows?"

"As long as we're on the road until Friday, let's go someplace interesting! Make him burn some gas and work a little for his money."

Mac tapped on the steering wheel. "You ever made sand castles? Really nice ones, not just the overturned bucket?"

"Can't say that I have! You?"

"There's a lady down on South Padre that teaches people how to do it. Let's go take a lesson!"

"You're on." She went back to the GPS. "When you get to the Interstate turn left... and about fifty miles later we'll turn south. Be there by ... oh, this will be a long drive. Let's just not stop!"

"I have to tell you ... any road trip through Texas requires a stop at Dairy Queen!"

"Need to brush up on your Peanut Buster Parfait skills?"

"You know me too well."

"Not yet, but I'm working on it!"

# Chapter 9

Snap parked and went into the range. He looked around, and noticed the signup sheet for the shooting lanes. Sure enough ... they had been here.

He eased up to the counter, and stared at the clerk, who came over in a couple of minutes.

"You had a couple here, 'Mac' and something, signed in about ten?"

Snap was sure from the clerk's expression that he remembered them, but he went to the signup sheet and looked it over.

"Yep, looks like it."

"Don't mess with me, kid. You remember them. When did they leave? Did they say where they were headed next?"

Chuck stepped back from the counter, removed the retainer strap on his holster, and without looking around, called "Charlie." Two men came from offices behind the long counter, and also loosened their sidearms. They stood behind Chuck off to each side, and watched.

"Your name?" said Chuck.

Snap looked at the men, and back at Chuck. "Does it matter?"

"If you're carrying a weapon, it needs to be unloaded, breech open. The sign outside said so. If you're armed, lift your shirt."

"Hey, man, I was just asking ..." He took a step backwards, and the three men behind the counter stepped further apart, each resting a hand on his sidearm. He lifted his hands in a motion of I-don't-want-no-trouble.

"You guys have a nice day, all right?" Snap turned, lowered his hands, walked slowly to the door, pushed it open, and stepped out.

All right. They were here. Don't need no help from those jerks anyway.

He stopped. Wasn't that Mac's truck, right in front of him? He pulled out some notes, and confirmed the license plate. So they're on foot, and right here. In a store somewhere?

He looked carefully up and down the street, looked back at the door to the range, and slipped a hand in his pocket. Walking slowly down the side of the F150, he knelt down briefly and reached underneath. Then he straightened up and continued across the street to the sidewalk on the other side.

He touched his pistol, made sure it was loose. But he couldn't do anything ... gotta wait until Friday. Or not. Would the boss care if he did the job early? Nah. Just get it done, who cares when?

He pushed open the door to the hardware store in the next block, and wandered in.

Gotta be careful. He might remember me. Didn't have a beard then... maybe not.

He looked down the aisles and found nothing.

"Can I help you?" A young brunette with a store name tag stood before him.

"Yeah. Got some nine mil shells?"

"Yes, sir. Range, or personal protection?"

"Yeah, those. Don't need no range stuff."

"Have a preference on brand?"

She led him to the back counter and stepped behind it. "We have Winchester, Remington, ..."

"The white box, that's good stuff. Two of them."

He laid a hundred dollar bill on the counter.

"Do you have anything smaller?" she asked, holding it up to the light.

"It's American money, girlie. Got a problem with it?"

"Let me check." She disappeared around the corner, and quickly came back. "This will be fine. But could I see some ID?"

"Good grief," he exclaimed, and took back the bill. "Never mind." He stomped out of the store, shaking his head. "Who are these people, anyway? Never seen any real money?"

He glanced back up the block, and saw that the truck was still there. Two blocks further a giant hamburger stared at him from a tall post, and his stomach spoke.

"Yeah. Sounds good. Let's do that."

He searched the sidewalk ahead of him and behind, and looked down the side streets, but no one was out in the heat. The sun reflecting off some of the store windows was blinding.

When he came out of the hamburger shop, the truck was gone. He ran to his car, threw it into gear, lurched into the street, and drove past the range. No sign of it ahead of him on the main road. He threw it around the corner to the right and again to the right, and got back to the main road going the other way. A mile or so down, he realized there had been a black pickup parked on that back street, around the corner from the range. Were they messing with him?

He bounced the car over a curb into a parking lot, spun around, ran back over the curb into the street, and accelerated back up the road. When he got to the place he had seen the truck, it was gone.

About eleven, Jennie pulled off the highway in San Antonio at the Huebner exit. Mac looked up from his iPad.

"Let's call it a day. There's a Marriott around the corner here."

A right on Fredericksburg and a left on Prue, and she pulled in.

"You see what's next door?"

Jennie glanced over to the right. "A police substation."

"And across the street?"

"Gold's Gym."

"Did you know they have racquetball courts?"

"Really! Ready for another lesson?"

He laughed. "Whenever you're ready, teacher! Maybe before breakfast?"

"Speaking of which — do you see what's across the street?"

The Cracker Barrel sign glowed against the black sky.

"I don't do hotel breakfasts when I can avoid it," she smiled, "but maybe you could buy me something interesting over there!"

She pulled into an open space and turned off the ignition. "But why were you interested in the police station?"

He stepped out and pulled a flashlight from the glove compartment. "Just curious ... since he was walking the street where we had parked ... "

A minute later he stood up from searching under the vehicle. "Here it is. He put a bug on us." He held out a small box for her to see. "Magnetic. Tells him where we are."

"What should we do with it?"

"I was thinking of sticking it to the exhaust pipe of one of those police cars."

When they checked out of the hotel the next morning and drove out onto Prue, Mac turned left past the police parking lot. "That one's gone. Hope it's a merry chase!"

"Where are you going? The Cracker Barrel is that way ..."

"There are Cracker Barrels everywhere. I need to introduce you to a famous pancake house, since you had the amazing good fortune to exit at Huebner!"

"Is there any restaurant in this whole country you haven't tried?"

"Maybe we'll find one! We've got a couple more days, remember?"

As the sun touched the horizon, they passed the Port Isabel lighthouse, drove up onto the Queen Isabella Causeway bridge, and coasted down onto South Padre Island. Turning left on the main road, they drifted a few blocks down, turned right, and again left on Gulf Boulevard.

"Gulf Boulevard?" asked Jennie. "I see the Gulf, but where's the Boulevard?"

Mac laughed. "Imagine two bicycles going each way. Four lanes. Doesn't that make a boulevard?"

"I like it already. Where are we staying?"

"The Sunburst I ... is there a II? ... III. There it is. Condos for rent. I called them yesterday, and they had one open. Used to come here as a kid. We need to drive by the rental office to get the key ... let's see, where's ... "

He fumbled in a shirt pocket. "Verna Jean Drive. Can't be far."

As they drove along looking for the turn, Jennie exclaimed, "Look! A full moon coming up over the surf!"

An hour later, they sat on the second story balcony watching that moon drift higher in the sky.

"You know," said Mac, "Ratface has no reason to wait four days, like What's His Name told me. If he's tired of the chase, he could try something anytime he wanted to."

"But he's still chasing cop cars around San Antonio, isn't he?"

"I figure by noon today he was back on our trail, and steaming mad."

"So we should set a trap."

"I like the way you think. Any ideas?"

# Chapter 10

Jimmy fished his phone out of the shirt pocket, turned it on, and flipped down the list. He touched a name, and put the phone to his ear.

"Snap. Jimmy. How's it going?"

Jimmy pulled the phone away from his ear and waited. When the cursing stopped, he brought it back.

"I gather he's giving you a little trouble."

"If you wanna check," said Snap, "that little tracker box of yours is now stopping jerks for traffic tickets somewhere in beeyootiful downtown San Antone."

"Really!" exclaimed Jimmy. "Why did you put it on a police car?"

"Don't gimme no 'why did you' bull! Your friend Mac put it there!"

"Ah, I think I understand. So ... do you know where he is now? And do you expect to catch up to him by Friday? Where are you, by the way? Taking some time to visit the Alamo?"

Silence.

"I gather that's a bad guess. All right, don't tell me."

"I'll tell you this," snapped Snap. "Ain't gonna wait for no Friday. Soon as I catch up to your gentleman friend, he's done."

"Now, Snap, that's hardly fair. I mean, we told him four days, after all."

"You told him four days. I didn't."

The phone went silent, and Jimmy looked at it. Sure enough, Snap was gone.

"It's just not fair," mused Jimmy. "But sometimes life is not fair."

He touched another name on the phone list.

"Rubio. Jimmy."

"Yeah."

"Snap is chasing a target for me, and having a little trouble."

"Yeah?"

"Got time to help him?"

"For?"

"How about ten? I think it'll come down in your neighborhood."

"Sure. Talk to me."

"Sounds like the chase just went through San Antonio. My guess is they're headed for the beach, which I think would mean South Padre. He likes that place."

"You're not talking about Mac, are you?"

"Why, Rubio, I am! How did you know?"

He held the phone away from his ear again, until the cursing died down.

"I gather you would be pleased to lend a hand in this project?"

"When?"

"I told Mac he would have until Friday to say his goodbyes. Our friend Snap may cut that schedule short a bit, if he can, so you might want to hurry."

"How do I find him?"

"Here's the license ... black F150 ... and if there's a Dairy Queen on the island, that would be a great place to watch."

"But you're welcome to call Snap," he added, "and tell him I asked you to help, and that his share is still his share. Find out what he knows. I'm sure he'll appreciate your help."

"Yeah, like a vulture would. That it?"

"That's it. No holds barred."

The phone went silent again. Jimmy smiled.

"Morning, Sunshine!"

Mac pulled the curtains open, and sunlight streamed into the bedroom. Jennie covered her head with a pillow.

"Think it's too early to call the sand castle lady?"

Jennie groaned, and stayed under the pillow.

"We don't have any supplies! No coffee, nothing! Forgot to go by the grocery store last night!"

"Give me a minute to shower," mumbled Jennie, "and we'll go find something."

"You do realize our first stop needs to be at the hardware store, right?"

"For what?" she hollered through the bathroom door.

"Tools! For carving sand castles!"

"What about shields, for warding off 9 mm shells?" she asked, coming out rubbing her hair in a towel. "He's going to find us pretty soon, right? Isn't that what you think?"

"Did I mention that we've met before, Ratface and I?"

"No! Over a card game at the club?"

"Did I mention I always lose at poker, so there are no card games, and there is no club?"

"No, but I'm delighted to know you always lose at poker! I can hardly wait! So, where did you meet this fine person?"

"He didn't have a beard then. Took me a while to realize that, and recall the right guy. Hired gun, ruthless, messy, nothing clever about him. Barge in, blow things up, sneak away — that's his style."

"So he knows you."

Mac smiled. "Yeah, and I would guess he grew the beard to hide some memories."

"So he likes you."

"I'm sure he does. Why, we're almost best friends. Almost.

Until he can get rid of me, and then he'll be delighted with our relationship."

"What about me?"

"You're new to him. Let's see .... he will assume you are helpless, and save his last bullet to make sure there are no witnesses left."

"Nice. A gentleman."

"Can't say that word would come to mind about him, no. Probably not."

"And how soon do you expect him?"

"By tomorrow. He knows we were in San Antonio, the bit with the police car will tell him we stayed at that hotel, and somehow he'll figure out we came this way. Tomorrow will be Thursday, the third day since the call, and he won't have any reason to wait until Friday."

"So today we can play in the sand. Let's go! I'll need a swimsuit, after breakfast, after the hardware store, and some sun lotion ... this will be fun!"

"Do you feel funny sitting out here on the beach in a Hawaiian shirt?"

"Not at all," said Mac, bending his head down almost to the sand to inspect the scallops under the first floor roof of his sand castle. "I'd feel funny if Ratface showed up and I didn't have the XD with me."

"Pass me the spatula, please?"

She carved a straight side down the drying mud pile. "Like this?"

"That's it. If you got the mud solid before it dried, no air pockets, then it'll be fine. Otherwise you have to get creative... nothing like an air pocket to inspire a second story balcony entrance to the castle!"

"Speaking of which..." she said quietly, looking back at the condominium. "There's someone in our apartment."

"Does he have a beard?" asked Mac, without looking up.

"I think so... but he's in housekeeping clothes."

"Pity the housekeeping person he got them from. Could you stand a lunch break?"

"I think so. Suddenly I can't stay focused on carving this sand ..."

"Yeah, my mind is wandering too. Let's wander back to the truck."

"Think he found it?"

"No, your idea about renting a garage in the next block was excellent. We might want to check at the rental office, though, and see if they did any damage there ... I assume he paid them a courtesy visit, just to ask how they were, how's business, all the usual stuff ... oh, and if you don't tell me where they are I'll shoot you. That sort of chit-chat."

When they walked into the rental office at Verna Jean Drive, no one was at the desk.

"Shhh..." said Mac. "Listen."

"Hello", he called, and in the silence they heard a soft thumping sound. They followed it to discover a young lady tied up in a closet with a man's tie wrapped around her head as a gag.

Jennie untied her and lifted her up, while Mac dialed 9-1-1.

"What happened?" asked Jennie, after settling the woman into a chair and assuring her the police were on the way.

"A man came in and put a chair under the doorknob," she said, motioning towards the entry door. "I was so surprised I just sat here, not knowing what to do, almost unable to move. He described you ... now that I see you in person ... and demanded to know where you were."

She closed her eyes and took some deep breaths. "I told him we don't share information about our tenants, and he grabbed the neck of my blouse and pulled me towards him, half way across the counter..."

She began to cry and tremble. Jennie pulled a chair up close, took her hands and cupped them in hers, and waited.

"It's OK," said Jennie when the woman looked up at her. "Here: tissues. Whatever you told him is fine, we're fine, and we'll let the police deal with it."

The door opened quickly and two policemen stepped in. Mac greeted them. "I'm the one who called; we found this young lady tied and gagged in a closet. We think the man who did it may have broken into our condominium about half an hour ago ... number 206, over at Sunburst III."

"Thank you. ID, please?" said one of the officers, while the other took Jennie's chair and began coaxing the story from the clerk.

"So, why do you think the same person is in your apartment?"

"He apparently assaulted her to find out where we were. And from out on the beach we saw someone in our balcony — someone who's been stalking us — so we came here to see if he had forced this office to tell him where we were. Looks like he had."

"Have you filed a complaint? About the stalking?"

"No, sir, we have not. Perhaps we could continue the conversation after you apprehend him? 206, Sunburst III?"

The other officer joined the conversation. "You called for an ambulance?"

"I did, officer — when we found her, I thought it best to be sure someone looked her over. No telling what he did to convince her to talk."

"Other than emotional shock, she seems unharmed, but that's a great thing to do. They are almost here — that's their siren you hear."

"Jim," said the first officer, "let's go get him. These folks have given us what we need."

"Jennie, you have your key? Officer, here's my key to the apartment, in case you need it. We'll come along a little bit behind you — just leave it on the counter, if you leave before we see you there."

The second officer seemed a little worried about leaving, but nodded to Jim and followed him out. The EMT medics came to the door as they left.

"Ma'am, I think you'll be OK now. We'll leave you in their hands. Just tell them what happened, and you can decide whether you'd like to have the ER check you over. And again... don't worry about us!"

Mac waved the EMT team on in, and took Jennie outside.

"Let's see ... we were talking about lunch ... I was thinking maybe Blackbeard's, but given the situation ... maybe not! I saw there's a BurgerFi here... ever been to one?"

An hour later, Jennie asked, "Should we go back to the apartment? Won't they be waiting for us?"

"No, I don't think they'll be waiting for us," laughed Mac. "If they caught him, they're busy booking him on several charges. But if they gave him any warning they were coming, he slipped away, and they would be back at the rental office by now."

"You think he got away, don't you?"

"I'm sure of it. He would have seen that squad car coming, as he watched for us to come back."

"So ..."

"I noticed a car rental place at the front of the island. Avis, I think. Let's get something he won't recognize, hide my truck, and rent a different condo. I have some more work to do on that castle!"

# Chapter 11

Mac dropped Jennie off at the Avis lot to rent a car, and drove back to park in the rented garage. The Dairy Queen caught his eye before he got there, and he pulled in.

It'll take her a few minutes to rent that car. I'll get a parfait to go, and have a few minutes to work on it before she gets there.

He glanced around the restaurant as he entered. Two or three people sitting around, but Ratface was not one of them. He waited at the counter until the clerk got free, and placed his order.

As he sat down, he noticed someone must have left; only two people remained, and they looked like they probably intended to spend the day. Not a bad idea.

He pulled a few napkins from the dispenser, wrapped them around the parfait, and carefully pushed the door open, watching for any dripping ice cream. He juggled the keys into his hand, unlocked the F150 ... I left it unlocked? ... And slid into the front seat.

As he awkwardly pulled at the seat belt with his free hand, Rubio slipped into the back seat from the other side, with a revolver pointed at Mac's head.

"Hey, Mac. Remember me?"

Jennie stepped inside the Avis office and got in line behind two other customers. Fifteen minutes later, her turn came.

"What's the most common thing you rent here?"

"Probably the Ford Edge, usually white."

"Got one?"

"Just for you. Drivers' license, please? Credit card? And will you buy gas before returning it?"

"No, you can fuel it up after the rental."

"And the insurance? If you have it ..."

"Sure," said Jennie, getting tired of the conversation. "I'll take the insurance. If I have it, and anything happens, I can just walk away, right?"

"Yes, ma'am, basically."

"Let's do it."

Thinking of Mac waiting for her outside that rented garage, she felt some anxiety about getting back there. The clerk walked around the car with her, and offered the pad for her signature. Jennie signed, took the pink copy and the rental receipt, and quickly pulled out onto Padre Boulevard.

When she got to the garage, Mac was not standing around waiting. She pulled up to the door and tapped the horn. Nothing happened.

She got out and knocked on the garage door. No answer.

She pulled her phone from her purse and touched his name on the display. He finally answered.

"Hello ... Jennifer. I ... stopped ... at ... the ... Dairy Queen ... and met ... an old friend."

Her blood ran cold. Struggling to keep her voice steady, she said, "So will I see you at the apartment?"

"Sure ... honey. See if ... our ... two friends ... from this morning ... got what they ... needed... OK? See you ... there."

And the phone disconnected.

OK. Our two friends.

She jumped into the car and drove back to the rental office. The police car had returned, but was just pulling away. She waved frantically.

Jim was driving, and pulled to the curb. She parked and ran to his window.

"They've got my husband. He was not where we agreed to meet, and I called him. He had gone to the Dairy Queen, and they grabbed him there ... I think they are taking him to the apartment, maybe to get me too."

Jim shook his head. "No one was there. Nothing had been disturbed."

"There must be two of them," said Jennie, almost to herself. "Only someone he didn't recognize could have gotten close enough..."

"Would you like us to follow you back there, ma'am?"

"No... if they see your car, they'll just kill him and run. And even if we go in this rent car, they'll see your uniforms... I think I've got to do it."

"Do what, ma'am?"

"Rescue him."

Mac looked back over his shoulder. "Rubio! Didn't know you liked the beach!"

"Yeah, I do. Lots of places to bury things."

"Really!" said Mac, turning back to face the windshield. "Got something you need to bury?"

"Maybe!" laughed Rubio. "You've got a condo or something here. Let's go there, have a little chat."

Mac's phone rang. "Excuse me for a minute, Rubio? I need to take this."

"Sure, old man. Just don't say anything rude about me. Bad manners, you know. And keep it short."

When Mac hung up, Rubio pushed the revolver barrel into his neck. "Go."

Mac drove slowly across the few blocks to the Sunburst, and eased into the last striped slot on the end. "I'm guessing our old friend Jimmy asked you to come say hello, and sent his greetings. Wished he could be here, and all that. Good guess?"

"Shut up and get out. Hands up."

Mac eased out of the car, hands up shoulder high. Rubio came out behind him and closed the rear door.

"Rubio, won't this look suspicious? Me holding my hands up like this?" He turned to face Rubio, raising his arms high over his head.

Rubio waved the revolver. "Put 'em down lower!" When Rubio waved the barrel away from Mac's face, Mac jumped into him, his left hand pushing the firearm away and his right fist following up with a jab into Rubio's nose and then a hard blow to the stomach. Rubio doubled over. Mac twisted his right arm further, forcing him down to the ground, and putting a knee into his back. He forced the gun back against Rubio's wrist until he let go.

"Drop it, Mac." The voice came from behind him.

Mac slowly turned to look, and discovered an excellent view of the wrong end of a .45 calibre automatic. Behind the firearm was Ratface.

"Snap! It's been a while! I was wondering if you were the one Jimmy sent! You've grown a beard!"

"Who's that under your knee?"

"Get off me!" screamed Rubio.

"Rubio? What are you doing here?"

Mac tossed Rubio's revolver under the car and stood up, facing Snap, who took a long step backwards.

"You got a room here? What number? Start walking. Slow."

Rubio crawled under the car to find his weapon, cursing, as Mac and Snap began a careful, step by step parade up the stairs and down the walkway to 206.

"Open it," said Snap when Mac reached the door. "Let's go in. We need to talk." As Mac turned the handle, something hit his head.

Jennie was at the corner two blocks away when she saw two men at the door to the room. She saw one of them fall. Then she saw a third man run up the stairs, and help drag the fallen man in. She parked at the other end of the building, ran the stairs two steps at a time as quietly as she could, then walked to the door.

What to do?

She knocked twice and called, "Housekeeping!"

"Go away!" said two voices.

She knocked again, louder. "Hola! Housekeeping!"

A voice much closer to the door said, "Go away!"

"Tengo qué limpiar!" she shouted, in as much of an accent as she could put together. "Es mi trabajo!"

The door jerked open and she lunged into the room, shoving the man with the black beard down on the floor. Behind him stood the second man, his pistol in her face. "Stop," he shouted.

The door swung closed behind her. She stopped. Snap climbed to his feet and swore at her. She did not see Mac anywhere.

"Get over there," said Rubio, motioning with his head. "Hands up." Snap shoved her along. As she came out of the entry hall and into the room, she saw Mac lying on the carpet unconscious.

"Snap. Go look outside." Rubio stood facing Jennie, holding her at gunpoint. "Make sure nobody else is coming!"

"Jim, we need to help her."

"And fast. But she's right - we can't go like this."

"Your house is closer than mine. Let's get some clothes, and then we can use your car."

Jim floored it, and the squad car was at his front door in two and a half minutes. They ran into the house, and Jim grabbed some jeans and a big T shirt. "Here, Chip, these will fit you. We're about the same size, close enough. Keep your belt and holster, just under the shirt."

They were changed and in Jim's family car in another six minutes, and speeding down the long road on the laguna side of the island. At the cross street Jim slowed down, turned, and drove to Sunburst III in what he hoped looked like normal speed.

"You still have the key?" asked Chip.

"Yeah, haven't had a chance to give it back."

"We may need it... we'll want to go in fast."

He parked at the north end of the building. "It's at this end, six doors down. 206. Ready?"

They gently closed the car doors and started up the stairs. As they stepped out onto the second floor walkway, a man with a black beard stood with his hand on the doorknob of number 206, looking around as though he were waiting for someone.

"That's him," murmured Jim. "Go past him, then turn back."

But as they approached, something about them caused Snap to react, and he bolted for the far stairway. As he ran, they both instinctively took up the chase. Jim ran after him, but Chip turned back and went down the stairs they had just come up.

When Jim got to the bottom of the other stairs, Snap had just closed the door on a black sports car, and a gun barrel was waving at Jim through the open window. He jumped back behind a support column, and the car lurched into the street, turning north. Chip came around the corner at the north end. Snap accelerated at him. Chip dove sideways to the concrete, out of the way. Jim ran out and focused on the license plate.

After helping Chip up, Jim repeated the license three or four times, hoping that between them they could remember it. "Here," said Chip, I've got my phone. Dictate it."

Then they looked upstairs. "Let's go check on things," said Chip, and Jim nodded. Chip was limping as they climbed the stairs again. At the top he stopped to lean on the railing.

"I need a minute to shake off that fall, Jim. Go on and check on them, and I'll call the plate in."

Jim went on to the door and knocked.

"Come in!" came a rough voice from inside, and not one Jim recognized. Not one he cared to meet, from the sound of it. He looked back and caught Chip's eye, and motioned with his head for Chip to follow him.

He turned the knob, and it opened. He stepped in, leaving the door ajar. Rubio stood there with his gun pointed at Jennie, who stood with her hands up, but not very far. She stayed focused on Rubio, who looked at Jim and said, "You get in here, too, jerk, and put your hands up!"

In the moment he turned his head and spoke to Jim, Jennie threw a kick that would make any dojo proud, and the firearm flew out of his hand. By the time he hollered, looked at her, and back at Jim, he was looking into a 9 mm barrel.

Jennie backed up and moved sideways to where the pistol had landed near the balcony. Without taking her eyes off Rubio, she said, "He was about to kill Mac."

"And the rest of you too!" shouted Rubio, pulling a second gun from his belt and pointing it at the officer. A gun fired from behind Jim, and Rubio fell backwards across the breakfast table. Jennie had Rubio's pistol by this time, and he found himself down three to zero with a hole in his shoulder. As he struggled to get up from the table, Jennie smashed the firearm handle across his forehead, and then gently handed it to Jim.

"Self defense, I'm sure you agree."

Jim took the gun and laughed, and turned to Chip. "Thanks, partner."

"You seemed to be hesitating, and ... well, I was next in line if he missed you!"

"Gentlemen, could I get a little help here?" said Jennie. "I don't think our gangster is going to wake up for a while." Together they lifted Mac onto the bed, and Jennie got a washrag and cold water to wash his face.

"Rubio," said Mac, opening his eyes. "His name is Rubio. A killer working for Jimmy Palacio."

"We got him, Mac," said Jennie.

"Ma'am, if you don't mind my asking," said Chip, "where did you learn that kick?"

"Oklahoma, I think," smiled Jennie. "No, wait, it was 'Anything Goes', the Cole Porter play ... or maybe ..."

"I got it," said the officer. "My daughter's a dancer, too. Well done!"

"But where's the black beard?" asked Jennie.

"He left. He was at your door when we got here. Took off, tried to run Chip over on the way. I guess we looked too much like what we are, even in these clothes."

"Thank you, gentlemen." Turning to Mac, she added, "I told them not to come in the squad car and uniforms... that Ratface would get hasty, and I had to come alone."

"Yes, thank you," said Mac, rubbing the back of his head and sitting up. "So Jimmy sent two. So far," he added, with a wink at Jennie. "We need to fix this. I'm tired of the game."

"The game?" said Jim.

"They said I had four days to live. That would have been tomorrow. If they're not even going to play fair, I'm done."

Rubio groaned.

Mac looked at him. "Shall I throw him off the balcony, officer, or do you want him?"

"I suppose I have to call an ambulance," muttered Jim.

"You know," said Jennie, "it's about time we left. Mac, can you leave them the other key? I think they still have mine."

"Sure, here you go." He tossed it onto the counter. "I'll grab a bag from the bedroom and we'll disappear."

"You don't want to press charges?"

"I think he attacked a police officer, and there was a witness," said Jennie. "Can't see that you need us for anything. I've got a rent car to return, and we've got some distance to go ... away from Ratface!"

"Agreed," said Mac. "Where I need to press charges is not in your jurisdiction. And I wasn't planning to, anyway. I need to come to an agreement with our friend Jimmy."

Jennie smiled at Jim. "Not an agreement you would care for, sir."

"Something tells me I'd like to watch, though! OK, Chip, let's get an ambulance on the way. Did you get the other guy's license called in?"

"Sure did."

"You have Snap's license?" asked Mac. "Let me write that down, if you would. And if you wanted to give the ambulance a wrong address ... maybe off the island somewhere? ... so this guy, Rubio, could lose a little more blood?"

A few minutes later they were turning in the rent car and driving towards the bridge.

"Mexico?" asked Jennie.

"No," said Mac. "They have guns down there. It's not safe."

# Chapter 12

Snap pulled into the driveway of a rundown beach house that looked deserted, and backed the car up towards the door. He got out, opened the trunk, and pulled out another license plate and a screwdriver. When he was finished, the old license plate was buried in the sand of an empty lot next door.

He drove back towards the bridge, and parked in a strip center parking lot where he could watch the cars leaving the island. In just a few minutes, his strategy paid off. He saw the black truck follow a white Ford Edge into the Avis lot, and a few minutes later leave that lot and drive out into the westbound traffic headed over the bridge.

After a few more cars went by, he pulled into the lane behind them.

Now what, mister? Think you can go somewhere I can't follow you?

At the lighthouse in Port Isabel, the pickup truck turned around and drove back onto the bridge. Snap went another block and did the same thing, now about fifteen cars behind them.

Just past the South Padre Island welcome sign, the pickup turned around again. Snap did the same, and there was no place to go a little further to make it less obvious.

What are you doing, bonehead? Can't find your way off the island?

Two blocks past the lighthouse, the pickup turned around again, and headed back east.

Last time, thought Snap. I'll blow your tires out!

When the truck turned around this time, a police barricade appeared between them, and another one suddenly blocked the road behind him. Mac's truck disappeared over the westbound bridge, and Snap saw police coming from both directions as he was forced to a stop.

Jimmy tapped a tango, or what he thought might be a tango, on the desktop. It was time for some good news, probably from the beach. Nothing. He thought a drive past the house might do him some good. Mac's house, not his. Just to look at the empty driveway, the empty house, and gloat.

Matter of fact, why not slip in and enjoy a beer or two? Watch a movie? No danger of them coming back, after all. Snap might fail, though he never did, and Rubio might ... though he never had ... but between them, it was done. And done far away. He loved it. Shouldn't be too hard to shut down the alarm system and just enjoy an evening ... drinking the enemy's wine and relaxing on his sofa.

Morning rush hour was fading as he pulled out of the underground garage past the debris and filth of an abandoned, industrial part of town. He drove a few blocks to the interstate entrance and gunned it up to 90, weaving around the idiots who thought speed limits mattered.

What's a car for, after all? Make it go, drink in the speed, leave everyone else drooling.

The sky was dark when he reached the long bridge over the lake, and then the turn into their neighborhood. The long way around, come up to the house from a side road. Drive by once, just to be sure... yeah, it's dark and empty. Nice. Permanently empty.

He pulled up to the curb around the corner in front of a "for sale" sign, walked back to the driveway, looked around, and walked slowly down the side of the house looking for the alarm wiring. Across the back, down the other side... didn't find anything. No stupid "protected by" sign in the front.

He slipped a knife blade in the door frame around the back door and slowly worked the bolt back into its slot. He eased the door open and listened. Nothing. Leaving the door slightly ajar, he walked back to his car and started Pandora's "Beethoven Moonlight Sonata" station. After a long adagio, and no police cars or sirens disturbing the peace of the evening, he decided there must not be an alarm system to worry about.

He walked back to the house, slipped in the back door, and turned on the kitchen light. What's in the fridge? Two cold beers and a blueberry pie, that's what.

Gotta be ice cream, with a blueberry pie. Yes, the best. Ah, what a smart man I am.

He found a spoon and made a couple of trips to get the beer, the pie and the ice cream to the living room. About a minute later the Broncos were chasing the Panthers across a wide screen TV, and the night was underway. With a good view out the living room window, he would not be taken by surprise.

"Honey, wait a minute."

Mac paused at the stop sign before their block.

"Did you leave the TV on?"

He looked at her and smiled. "Since I met you, who has time for TV?"

"It's on."

He looked down the block and saw the glow of the big screen reflecting on the curtains of the living room.

"Sure enough, we have company! Must not have those wireless alarms set up right."

"This is ridiculous!" she replied. "Let's finish the game!"

They parked a couple of blocks away and walked towards the

house.

"No car in the driveway. Where do you think it is?"

"Not far ... just a minute, I need my tools." Mac returned in a minute, tossing a roll of duct tape in the air. "Yeah, I think I got everything."

"Great. I nominate that car, by the "for sale" sign. What do you think?"

"Might be. Wanna bet it's still warm?"

Touching the hood, Mac said "I give it an hour at most. Not enough time to drink all our beer, but probably enough time to do serious damage to the leftover ice cream!"

"But who?"

"We left Ratface in the barricades, and Rubio in the hospital ... must be the boss! So sure of himself he decided to come visit. You think?"

"No better idea. Did you tell me you were this popular, when we met?"

"Slipped my mind ..."

"Here, toss me the roll while you hold one end." She walked around to the other side of the car, and in a minute the windshield was covered.

"A ball of it in the gas filler?"

"Of course. Headlights?"

"And the side mirrors... but that leaves him the rear view, so we'd better do the back window too. Can we get inside?"

"No, that'll be enough," said Mac. "Rather not risk an alarm going off."

Half a roll later, they were done. "Let's go make friends."

They came up to the house along the edge of the back yard. Through the kitchen window they could see him on the couch in the living room. The refrigerator door and the freezer door were standing open.

"No manners at all," she whispered.

"But he left the back door open for us," said Mac.

"Us and half the mosquitoes this side of the Mississippi, probably!"

"Got any spare pillowcases?"

"Might could find one, if you'll let me slip past you down the hall."

"OK, but don't disturb him as you go by."

"No, of course not."

Jennie ghosted through the kitchen, into the hallway, and disappeared. Mac stood in a darker corner of the kitchen where the refrigerator light did not reach him. He could see the television screen and Jimmy's reflection in the front windows. Jennie reappeared with a large, dark blue pillowcase. Mac nodded and took it from her.

When the police found him, Jimmy was lying on the lawn of the police substation, his head covered in a pillow case, his wrists taped together behind his back, and his ankles taped together all the way up to the knees. He had no identification, and his pockets were full of .45 calibre ammunition. There was a smell of beer about him, and what seemed to be blueberry pie and ice cream all over his shirt.

His keys were never found, and the car was towed the next day.

A week later, Jimmy was lying on the couch when the phone rang.

"Boss ... Rubio."

"Where have you been?" demanded Jimmy. "Why didn't you take care of business?"

"I'm in the hospital in Brownsville. Texas."

"Why, because you fell off your bike?"

"That's where they put people with bullets in their bodies."

"Rubio, you're confused. We put bullets in other people's bodies. We don't have bullets in our bodies. When you get that clear, come see me ... but until then, don't bother!"

He slammed the phone back in the base unit. "Good grief!"

The phone rang again.

"What?" he hollered.

"Boss ... it's Snap."

"You too? Are you in the hospital too?"

"No, boss ... but I need some bail. They want a lot, I ain't got enough, and I can't get out."

"Anyone who can't do a simple job needs time to think. So think. And when they let you out, think some more. And don't call me, I'll call you. Or not!"

Again, he jammed the phone into the charger. "Good grief!"

"So," said Mac, rolling over and stretching the next morning. "Did that give you something to write about?"

She looked up from her pillow and yawned. "No, of course not."

"Why not?" he gasped, in mock amazement.

"Because it happened. You can only write fiction, if you want to get fifty thousand words in a month! Anything else and you have to get it right. And what happened is ... well, it's not fiction!"

"If you told someone what we've been through since Monday, would they believe you?"

"No, of course not."

"Well, there you go! Fiction."

She tossed the pillow on top of him and climbed out of bed. "I need to write. I lost three days! Four!"

"But first..." he said, "you need breakfast. And I know this Cracker Barrel..."

# Chapter 13

"So choose your project," said Dr. Sorenson on the first day of class, "and let me know by next Monday what it is. Needs to require investigation, and you will create software to gather data and produce recommendations. This is called "data science," and you'll thank me forever if you decide you like it!"

Now what? thought Celena. I need a project and a programming language!

"Sal, what should I do? I'm not a programmer."

"Python is easy to learn," replied the student next to her. "That and 'R' are the two big languages in data science, and Python does lots of other stuff besides. Great choice for a math major, and especially one pretending to be an economist."

OK, then. Python.

And she began looking up ebooks. The Dummy's Guide to ... Learn in 24 hours ... Automate the Boring Stuff ... that sounds good ... a lot of choices!

She settled on "The Python Apprentice", and marked one about "Python and Data Science" to pick up next.

Looks easier than Java, and more fun than Fortran. This can work. But I need a project.

By the following morning she had settled on predicting stocks, the golden standard of goals that no one expects you to accomplish.

Jennie turned the latch and pushed the glass door open. The fluorescents high above flickered and came on. Celena dropped her bag outside the court, dug out her shoes, and sat down to pull them on.

"Nice court," said Jennie. "Not all scarred up like the others."

"Too bad," called Celena. "I depend on those marks to distract you, or hide the ball. Anything that will help!"

"Not today!" Jennie tossed a hot pink ball against the side wall and stroked a smooth backhand into the corner. "Ah, not today. That felt good." She caught it, set it up again, and lobbed it to the front of the ceiling.

"Here we go!" said Celena, closing the door behind her and swinging at the ball while it was still shoulder-high. It skipped on the plywood just before the front wall.

"Not percentage racquetball, that shot. Tough to make it work," said Jennie, as she scooped it up and punched a z-serve into the right wall. "Playing to 15?"

"Let's do a couple to 21, I'll have more time to catch up!"

They both laughed, and Jennie bent down to serve.

An hour later Celena collapsed against the side wall, flushed and breathing hard.

"Whew. Good workout!"

"Me too. Stretch out, I'll get the water bottles." Jennie brought the drinks in and sat down beside her. "So what else is going on in your life, besides teaching me Spanish and learning how to dig line drives out of the backhand corner?"

"Your Spanish is better than my defense, ¡no hay duda!" Celena took a long drink. "Well, I'm working on a fun project — predicting stock prices!"

"But you're in the math department ... isn't that more an economics deal?"

"I'm taking macro from Dr. Sorenson. An elective. And it's kind of a mathematical analysis problem, really."

"So, can you do it? Make you rich!" winked Jennie.

"No one does it very well, but it's been fun. And if you cheat a little, you can do it really well!"

"What do you mean? How would you cheat?"

"Well, if I guess that you're going to serve into my backhand corner, and just as you swing, I jump that way, I have a much better chance of returning it. Right?"

"And if you guess wrong?"

"Oh, no doubt, the point is over. I'll never make it back. But if I could look just a few seconds into the future and know which way you're going... why, I might actually win a game now and then!"

"Or if I had the flu. That might help you, too, and that might actually happen! But ... seriously ... look into the future a few seconds?"

"I'm analyzing historical data. So the truth is already known. It's just a question of whether the software, the program, knows the answer..."

"So you let it peek ahead."

"Exactly."

Jennie leaned back against the wall and closed her eyes. "Just don't ever present it as real."

"I know, I know. It's a fun problem, though... and sometimes I can get pretty close!"

Jennie stood up. "Got a few more minutes? Let's see how close I can get you to the front wall!"

Philip Cross stared at the screen. What was she doing?

Celena pointed to her notes. "Here's the formula, I just don't see how to do it in Python. Do you see what's happening?"

Philip studied her notes, then looked back at the screen. "This is a mess. How did you get this far as a math geek and not learn any more about programming?"

"FORTRAN. 'Formula Translator.' Been around a long time.

I'm good at it. Or, I was. Just haven't taken the time to learn Java, or this new stuff."

"The "new" stuff? Gosling dreamed Java up in, what, '94? '95? And Guido what's-his-name created Python before that! I thought FORTRAN had gone the way of COBOL and, you know, Visual Basic?"

"Philip. Please. Doesn't the business world still run on COBOL? And most of what us non-programmers use to talk to Oracle is really Visual Basic? You just won't admit it. Now how do I do this recursive thing so it works?"

Philip drained the styrofoam cup. "More, please? I'm a gallon short of my daily requirement!"

She laughed and went to find the Keurig brewer.

Forecasting stocks? How can that work? he wondered. What she was trying to do here wasn't hard ... take him a minute to unscramble the index ... indices ... in her loops, but no big deal, she just had it backwards. But what was she really doing?

"OK, I think we got it," he said, when she returned. "Two sugars, no cream?"

"Yup. You're done? You're already done?"

He smiled. "Thanks. I'll take that as a compliment."

"But that means I already had ninety percent of it, right?"

"Yes... you had ninety percent of it right."

"Thank you. Want to see what it does?"

Absolutely. He nodded, getting up and moving to her chair so she could settle in at the keyboard.

"Here's the historical data." She opened a text file and let it stream across the screen. "Economic data, start/stop and average values of hundreds of stocks, world event indicators, temperature - it affects demand for lots of things - other weather factors, everything I could think of that might drive stock prices."

He stared.

"So I'm in Sorenson's class, macroeconomics, not the beginner stuff, and I thought this would be a kick. See if I could squeeze the golden goose and get the egg everyone wants - accurate stock predictions!"

"OK ... " His measly investment in Worldcom had evaporated, so he understood the wish. If only he had put the money in Walmart, but he had thought he understood the tech world. It was the larger ocean, the one called economics, that his stock had drowned in.

"All right. Pick a stock, and the day you want to forecast."

"The day?"

"Sure, why not? If you can't predict both the value a stock will reach, and the day it will get there, what's the use?"

"Well... Walmart. Next Monday."

"No, silly, pick a date in history."

"But then you already know the answer!"

"But the program doesn't. We'll feed it the data coming up to that date... let's say, a month before the date you pick... and see if it can tell us what the number was going to be."

"Oh, I understand. And if it can predict stuff in history, you assume it can predict the future. Like, next Monday."

She nodded.

"Let me see some history on Walmart. Can you do that?"

"Sure, let's just use Ameritrade's screens."

She pulled up Firefox and logged into her stock account. "What date are we sneaking up on?"

"My birthday — April 11, last year."

She pulled up the history of WMT.

"How old are you?"

"Twenty. You?"

"Not supposed to ask a woman."

"Only fair. You?"

"Twenty-six. Late start."

"I would have guessed nineteen, maybe twenty!"

"Racquetball. Jennie and I play all the time!"

"Jennie ... really? Teaches journalism? She scares me ..."

"Why? She's funny, and really smart."

"Yeah, well ..." He drained the cup. "So confident. So sure of herself. Can you imagine her being afraid of anything?"

"I guess not," laughed Celena, "but if you could hit a kill shot like she does, you'd be confident too!"

"Let me get one more cup," he said. "Then you can show me your stuff. Want some?"

# Chapter 14

Celena chose a range of history leading up to Philip's last birthday, and picked a date a month after that to target. She printed out the graph of those dates for him to study, and booted up her software. By the time she had entered the key data, he returned.

I wonder if he'll see it.

"Have a seat," she said, still amused by his comment about Jennie. "Showtime."

He pulled the chair up and took the printed sheets from her.

"OK, I see. What date are you going to predict?"

"Right here," she said, reaching over and circling the data point. "And we'll let it study the data right up to ... here, your birthday."

He looked at the paper, then at her screen. "Let her rip."

"It may take a while," she said. "That's a lot of data, and some new kid just had his hands in the software." She hit the return key.

"What?" he said, acting shocked.

"It's done."

"What?" he said, looking back at the screen as it blinked $55.25 at him.

"What does the history say?"

He looked at the chart. "Not a dollar different."

"High or low?"

“You were high, about fifty cents.”

“OK.” She called up a screen full of settings and adjusted something, hoping she was quick enough that he could not follow what she was doing. “Let's run it again.”

He stared at the screen. Within a second it flashed “$54.82.”

He looked back at his chart. The stock was rising quickly in that time, and she had caught the price like a bear catches a salmon jumping through the falls. He looked at her without speaking.

“Good, huh?”

“No, you missed it by two cents.” After a moment, he said, “Let me guess. If you adjust things a bit more, you can nail it, and you can do it every time.”

She relaxed. “Yup.”

“So you're cheating.”

“Yup.”

“How?”

“I let the program peek ahead.”

He sat back in his chair and rubbed his face. “So it's a joke.”

“Well, a prank, anyway.”

“Are you going to turn that in?”

That was the question, she thought. How far to take the joke without getting caught, or worse.

“Maybe.”

“They'll flunk you.”

“Only if they catch me!  If it's never quite that accurate, but only good enough to look promising, I can get funding!”

“At some point, you have to predict real future values.”

She nodded. That was a bridge she would need to cross, if it became more than a prank.

"Maybe it's like guessing which way a Russian sub will turn at the bottom of the hour. You only have to be right once!"

“Good movie," said Philip, "and it worked for him! Listen, I've gotta go. Does anyone else know about this?”

"Only you," she said.

And Jennie. But why mention that?

Dr. Sorenson looked up. A Tuesday/Thursday student from the math department was at the door.

"Yes... Celena. Come in. The projector is there, so plug in at that end. I'll dim the lights when you're ready."

Celena unpacked her laptop and notes, and set things up without speaking.

"Do you have the Apple connector for the VGA port?"

She nodded, without looking up.

They're always nervous, he thought. Should be - half their grade riding on a single project!

Celena sat down, opened the laptop, and they both watched the projector image "Searching for input ... Computer found ..." and up came the Mac desktop background and dock.

"Well, tell me what you've done. What's the goal, how far did you get, etc."

She cleared her throat.

"I've created a program that predicts stock values."

He laughed.

"That's a good match for a math major in a macroeconomics course! But do you have the programming background for that?"

"A lot of Fortran work, and Philip ... Cross?"

Sorenson nodded.

"He helped me with the Python libraries and recursion routines."

"OK, be sure to note that assistance in your final write-up."

"Yes, sir."

"So... how far did you get?"

"Works pretty well. I have several years of historical data, and I'm running it against ..."

"Wait. Build it up for me. What data are you analyzing, why, how … all of it. Your understanding of the economics involved is my concern, remember!"

An hour later, he was ready. She took a deep breath, and waited.

"Take about three years of history, up to the first of this year, and make a guess on some of the big name stocks on … oh, May 15."

She chose GM, GE, and Apple, and ran the test.

"That's … impressive. You're within a few percentage points on every one of them. Is that a common result?"

"Sometimes it's better."

"What data has the most impact on the accuracy of the projections?"

"Industry averages, economic indicators like housing starts, the Fed policy on interest rates and monetary control… temperature is interesting…"

"Why?"

"A lot of key liquids are stored and used at different rates based on ambient temperature, and those usage rates drive supply and demand for the commodity liquids and related assets and services. So weather forecasts are monitored pretty closely by companies that store and transport those things, like Air Liquide, Air Products, Praxair, etc."

"Well, you seem to know your stuff. Want to show this off?"

"Umm …"

Her mind blanked. Her nerves screamed "No!" but apparently her mouth did not get the message.

"I'll book you for the faculty meeting next Thursday. Don't go into all the background, but … oh, half an hour should be fine, and demonstrate a few searches. We can take nominations from the floor on stocks to predict and the times involved…"

His phone rang. He looked at the display.

"Celena, forgive me. I need to take this, and it will be a long call. Go ahead and pack up, and - thank you. Very impressive. I'll send you the schedule."

He turned back to the phone.

"Yes, Dr. Wiggins, thank you for returning my call. Did my secretary forward you to this extension? Good. Tell me your analysis of the Fed's actions this morning."

# Chapter 15

The following Thursday Dr. Sorenson met her at the door to the faculty conference room. Fifty people or more were already milling about, and he hurried her to the podium.

“Plug your video in here. Power is there. When it’s our turn, I’ll introduce you so you’ll have time to open up the notebook and get everything ready. It doesn’t project for everyone to see until you throw this switch. Got it?”

She nodded, and began plugging things in. Dr. Sorenson turned to someone trying to get his attention, and when everything was ready she wandered over to the coffee bar.

“Celena?”

She turned and stood facing Dr. Louise Abrams, her major professor. “What brings you here?”

“Dr. Sorenson wanted to show everyone the project I’m working on for his macro class.”

“Wish you’d told me! What is it?”

“Stock price prediction algorithms.”

Dr. Abrams stared.

“It’s really a mathematical problem ...” she began lamely, but Dr. Abrams held up a hand. “It’s far more than that. How have you built anything substantial enough to show this group in one semester? And what did you write it in... Fortran? That’s all you know, best I recall.”

“I ... I got some help. It's written in Python, and... ”

“All right. They’re about to start. Needless to say, I’m very interested in seeing what you have done." Dr. Abrams turned and walked up the side aisle to a seat in the back of the mini-auditorium, and the lights dimmed enough that Celena could not see her face.

She put down the coffee and poured a glass of water instead. Last thing I need is more caffeine, she thought, as Dr. Sorenson came to get her.

"They've put us on first. Ready?"

She nodded. Liar, she thought. I'm nowhere near ready. What have I gotten into?

Dr. Sorenson stepped up to the podium, motioning to Celena to wait on the edge of the spotlighted area.

"Thank you for the opportunity to present some work by Celena Gris, one of Dr. Abrams' students ..."

He waved to her, and she lifted a hand in response.

"... who is taking my Macroeconomics 312, and has been doing some work on one of the hardest things known to mankind: predicting stock prices."

The audience laughed and began applauding. Dr. Sorenson turned to Celena and motioned her to come up with him. "Everyone in this room would now like to be your consulting client, and they are ready to pay dearly for your services," he laughed. "Amen!" came a deep, rough voice from the back of the room, and the laughter began again.

"Fire it up," Dr. Sorenson whispered, and stepped back off the simple stage. "It's all yours."

She looked out over the suddenly silent room and felt her blood pressure drop. She gripped the sides of the podium and watched her laptop screen until it sat waiting on her. She reached out, flipped the switch that revealed the projection image to the audience, and looked up.

"I'm ... very nervous," she said, and took a long drink.

"Well. You know how difficult it is to predict the stock prices far enough in the future ..."

"Sometimes it doesn't need to be very far, to save your fanny!" said someone in the first row. Many people chuckled, obviously in agreement.

" ... to be useful, and many factors impact it. Some of them I've studied are listed here."

The Powerpoint changed to a bulleted list of twenty items.

"And the full list requires 6 point type to fit on a slide!"

A screen full of tiny print emerged.

"But in our few minutes this morning, I won't dive into the background, except to say that the program I've built — with some programming help from Philip Cross in the Computer Science program — considers many social, economic, financial, and even meteorological factors, as well as the historical data on hundreds of stocks."

She switched from the Powerpoint to the live code.

"Dr. Sorenson suggested we might ask for stocks you are interested in, and demonstrate analysis of those stocks over particular time periods. For example, if you were investing in gold — say, GLD — as it had run up from 115 to about 180..."

She entered the relevant dates.

"And would care about the price a few months later ..."

"You're killing me," groaned the voice in the first row. Everyone laughed.

"Let's pretend we were here," as she pointed at the historical timeline, "and predicting the price... here." The stock had dropped 30 points by that time.

She entered the dates to review, and the date to predict, all displayed in text big enough for everyone to see.

"Now, let's see what it can do. My apologies, it may take a while." She hit the return key, and three seconds later the forecasted price displayed.

"And the real number was?"

She switched the screen to a table of data, scrolled down to the targeted date, and over to the GLD column. The prediction was off by eighty cents.

"Look at GM, middle of 2009, as though you had just cast your ballot in November 2008," shouted someone, and applause ran around the room.

"Actually, the government taking over General Motors was slightly outside the scope of what I got to this semester!" she protested. "I'm sure it would miss by a mile!" But it didn't.

"Apple." "Exxon." "Hewlett-Packard." "Valero." "CVS." Companies from every major industry were named, and finally Dr. Sorenson stepped up.

"We've more than used our allotted time, ladies and gentlemen. Thank you for participating so eagerly. I'll be taking a 4% commission on all net proceeds ... no, no, not really, I'm joking. Not enough of you laughed, so now I'm worried!"

He turned to Celena, who was hurriedly disconnecting and packing up. "Thank you, Celena." He turned off the microphone. "We'll talk."

"So will we," said Dr. Abrams, coming up to the podium. "Celena, can you be at my office about 3 tomorrow afternoon?"

"Yes, ma'am."

At three o'clock Friday Celena stood at her door in the math department, and Dr. Abrams motioned her in.

"Please, sit down, here at the table. Got your computer? Good. Show me your code."

"Ma'am?"

"Show me your code. I want to see what you've done."

"But it was for a course in Dr. Sorenson's department..."

"I am responsible for your completion of all requirements for a degree. Do you understand?"

"Yes, ma'am."

"Show me your code." She watched as Celena slowly opened the laptop and brought up TextMate.

"You're programming in TextMate?"

"Yes..."

Dr. Abrams said nothing, and Celena opened the “main” file.

She's working in a text editor, not even a serious programming IDE. Either she got a lot more help than she's admitting, or ...

"Which version of the interpreter are you using?"

"I'm sorry?"

"The interpreter. Which one are you using? And which statistical libraries?"

"Um... I'm sorry, ma'am, I don't know."

"Who did your Python work?"

"I did most of it, and Philip Cross helped with the recursion routine... I couldn't get the variables to work right, and I thought I had copied the source code correctly..."

"From?"

"From the Comp Sci 308 textbook."

"Go ahead. Show me the code."

Celena offered her the laptop with the code displayed, and she scrolled through it.

"Are all the files in this same module?"

"Yes?" Celena offered, obviously not sure what the question meant. Dr. Abrams opened Finder and verified that all the “.py” files were right there to be examined. She pursued the code down various branches of routines calling other routines, and finally was staring at what had to be the core engine.

This code is not doing what she said in the meeting. It can't be. There aren't enough variables, there's no code doing multivariate analysis... it's just not here.

"What is this routine, peek.py, doing? Looks like you give it a period of time, some number of days, and it simply goes that much further into the historical timeline data and retrieves a value."

Celena stared at her.

Dr. Abrams stared back, waiting, and suddenly she knew the answer.

"You're cheating. You can predict any price, at any time in the historical data, and you can't predict the price of mud in the real world."

Celena leaned back and said nothing.

"Tell me I'm wrong, Celena. Show me the code that does all that economic and meteorological analysis. Please."

Celena put her face in her hands, and finally looked up. "I can't."

Dr. Abrams picked up the phone and dialed 6 digits.

"Dr. Sorenson?"

Celena sat quietly in Dr. Sorenson's office as he filled out form after form. He was obviously enraged, and had hardly spoken to her after demanding confirmation of Dr. Abrams' conclusions.

"Leave your laptop here."

She began to protest.

"No, you cannot take it with you. It is school property, everything on it is school property, and you are no longer a student at this school."

It can't be. Not that fast, that suddenly.

"If you want to appeal, the instructions are here, but you will have absolutely no support from either me or Dr. Abrams, and the Dean will know the story in about an hour. Good luck getting his support."

"Be out of your dorm room by tomorrow at noon, and leave your key and student card in Dr. Abrams' office before you leave the campus tomorrow. No refunds will be offered for any of your fees, and no references will be provided by this school to other institutions you may consider. Your email account is already turned off."

He looked at her. "Not a pretty situation, but ... not our fault."

Standing up, he handed her a pair of identical forms.

"Read this, sign both copies, and we're done."

She looked them over, signed, and looked up at him.

"I'm sorry, Dr. Sorenson."

"Me, too. And thoroughly shamed in front of my peers."

She nodded. "Again, I'm sorry. It was a prank, and I never wanted to show it to all those people. You know I'll lose my visa, and have to go back to Venezuela."

"Lo siento," he said. "Goodbye."

# Chapter 16

Philip Cross flipped through screens of Java subroutines, smiling.

Good stuff. I think it's actually working. Well enough to show someone, anyway!

He fired it up, picked a date and a stock symbol at random, and set it to work. A list of filenames marched up and filled the screen, filenames being pushed off the top by more coming from the bottom. Files being absorbed, reviewed, filtered by the program. Files on his computer, files in the cloud, information from everywhere. 'Big data,' rivers of data carrying hundreds of factors to filter through, feeding the Java code looking for the key drivers that were moving this particular stock.

The screen began to fill with a floating list of key words being harvested from the raw data, words naming the factors being assigned the most weight. A converging set of vertical arrows drifted towards each other across the display. As though reluctantly drawn by a magnet, the arrows moved towards the center, coming together over a row of numbers sliding back and forth across the bottom of the screen. The numbers began as hundreds, then became whole numbers, then acquired decimal places. Two decimal places. Dollars per share. Stock prices.

Have to make it obvious the software is working hard, of course. Can't just show a blank screen, and then suddenly an answer. No one would trust it.

If only Celena could see this. Of course, she'd throw her

computer at me, for even thinking about doing... what she tried to do, and got thrown out for!

The arrows came together into a single arrow. A white circle formed and tightened, becoming center stage as the numbers auditioned for the lead role in this financial drama. Each number claiming that special place took on a red glow for the moment.

"17.23" moved into the center of the display. The row shifted a little, then a bit more, wavered for a moment among numbers within a few cents of that number, and settled into "17.19" as a final choice. The arrows vanished, and the prediction stood alone, bold and steady in the spotlight.

Dr. Sorenson strolled into the conference room. "Thanks again for all your help with the Economics students, Phil. I keep being surprised that a code jockey would have so much interest in macro, but you've been a great help in their projects."

"It's been fun, and they're a good bunch. Doing some nice work." He closed the browser.

"Yeah. Good. Well, what's up? You wanted to talk?"

"Let me show you something."

Half an hour later, Philip sat back and waited. Dr. Sorenson was quiet for a minute.

"You got this from Celena, didn't you?"

"Well, the idea," said Philip. "Her code was all on that laptop, and this is in Java, not Python. But it was an interesting challenge... and I've worked on it a bit."

"No kidding. If I hadn't been on this horse once before, and been thrown, I wouldn't have any idea what's under the covers. You know I threw her out of school because of it."

"Yeah, I warned her that turning it in as something real would not be a great idea."

"It wasn't. And I trusted her, so I got burned too. Lesson learned."

"But if you do real analysis, and take out the cheating code, guess what?"

Sorenson looked at him.

“It works.”

“I don’t believe you.”

“Pick a stock, and pick a date ... in the future.”

Dr. Sorenson chose Dell Computers three days later. The program hit it within 5%. He then asked for ERP, a pipeline company, one week in the future. Philip said it would rise 5%. Without telling Philip, Dr. Sorenson bought 100 shares on margin, and made $230 on the trade when it settled. He asked for a series of predictions a week or two out, and secretly placed margin orders, clearing over two thousand dollars in all.

"Philip," he said next time they talked, "so far we have been testing stable stocks; try something that is wildly changing, something that could easily go dramatically up or down."

Philip looked through the recent historical data for hundreds of stocks. "Here's a commodity ETF that was created in 2008, has a ten percent return over its life, but has gone from $60 to $15 in the last six months. If it were about to rise, it could be dramatic... let's see... I'll run it for the end of next month."

A moment later Philip whistled. "Wow. The program thinks it will be at $36 in six weeks ... over 100% growth from where it is now.

"OK, let's watch it. What's the symbol?"

Dr. Sorenson hurried home and connected to his brokerage account. He placed sales orders on all his current stock positions. Three days later he took all the available balance on two credit cards, most of what was in his checking account, and the proceeds from his stock holdings, and bought ten times that much of the commodity ETF "on margin", borrowing short term money from the broker.

Six weeks later the stock had fallen so far it could not be found with a shovel and a miner's helmet. The margin call would put Dr.

Sorenson into bankruptcy and destroy his career. There was no option. He dialed the number.

"Loans."

"Uh, I need to ... what interest rate are you charging?"

"If you have to ask, you're not desperate enough. Call when you're desperate." Click.

He called back.

"This is ... Doc. I need about half a million. What's the rate?"

"Come sign the papers. Do you know where we are?"

"No."

"That's because we're invisible. Park your car in the Walmart lot and stand at the sign that says "No dogs on grass." Frank will pick you up; he'll drive a black Lexus with a license that says, 'PAY NOW.' Can you be there at noon?"

"Sure..."

Click.

Dr. Sorenson closed the laptop, pulled the blinds, and turned off the lights in his apartment. He slumped into the recliner, turned off the TV, and leaned back, staring at the ceiling. This could be bad. What could he do? The only thing worse than paying off these guys would be not paying them off. But he had to pay the brokerage house, and his debt had to be secret. And the reason for the debt certainly had to be secret ... if anyone found out he had trusted this software a second time it would be ... he could not bear the thought.

He needed to raise funds. What about an appeal for angel funding? Get some venture capital people in a room somewhere, show the stuff, do something to give them confidence in its ability to actually look into the future, get a million or so, pay off "Guido," and skip the country.

Mérida. That would work.

A scam artist? An extortionist? Had he become no better than ... never mind what. There had to be a way out!

# Chapter 17

"Jennie?"

"Yes?"

"This is Dr. Sorenson, in the Economics department. Are you busy?"

"Just finishing some things, so I can make some time. What can I do for you?"

"I'd like to come see you for a few minutes."

"Sure, come on over. Meet you at the Coke machine downstairs?"

"No ... let me just come find you in your office. Kind of private."

"OK. Give me ten minutes, and come on over!"

She set the phone back down. This must have something to do with Celena, but did Dr. Sorenson know we were friends? Didn't think so ... there was nothing Jennie could have done when Celena was kicked out, so she did not reveal the relationship. Hmm.

Maybe he needed a piece written for something? No, that would not be 'private'.

Fifteen minutes later Dr. Sorenson was at the door.

"Come in, come in," she said. "Excuse the mess. Journalists are almost as bad as economists."

She winked at him and he laughed. "So you've seen my office!" he retorted. "They excavated two grad students last week ... lost them in 2012! I gave them both passing grades — for sheer endurance, you know — and sent them home to mama."

She poured coffee for both of them. "Cream? Sugar? Pink, yellow, blue, green, orange, or brown sweetener?"

He shook his head. "Aren't free markets amazing? Without them, you end up standing in a line around the block hoping the store has any bread at all, and with it, we have many choices in even the simplest things."

"Hmm. I could write a story on that," mused Jennie. "But that's not why you're here. What's up?"

He stood, closed the office door, and returned to his seat.

"I need your help and it has nothing to do with your job here."

Jennie sipped coffee and waited. Sorenson was single, as far as she knew, known as a successful investor, a respected instructor. Probably not a racquetball player, but he might shoot skeet. Why is he here?

"I need you to protect someone."

"Really? Do I have that reputation?"

"Am I mistaken? You do that kind of work from time to time, right?"

She nodded. If he was offering no insight into how he learned that, she would offer no credentials or examples. "Who's in trouble?"

"One of our students. Philip Cross. Do you know him?"

"I know who he is. As far as I know, we've never spoken. But he's in Comp Sci, isn't he? Not in your area?"

"True," nodded Dr. Sorenson. "But I've sponsored him to speak at a conference, and I'm ... for reasons I can't really go into ... I'm concerned for him."

"Concerned? For his safety?"

Dr. Sorenson looked into his coffee cup for a moment, then looked up. "I think he might be in danger of ... of being kidnapped. Certain people might think what he knows is valuable, and want it for themselves."

"What kind of knowledge? Don't tell me exactly, of course, but ... I want to know a little more about what we're dealing with, and what kind of people might be interested."

"Stock predictions." She stared. He smiled sheepishly. "I know, I know... this should sound somewhat familiar!"

"I was in the room when Celena Gris presented her work. Is this ... related?"

"Same idea," he admitted. "Philip has built his own version, done a lot of work on it, and has gotten it working. I'm not going to associate my name with it — again — for obvious reasons, but ... yes, the same stuff, and he's taken it forward a long ways."

"Who knows about it?"

"No one here, I would guess. And no one at the conference would know him from here."

"But the people there will be — let me guess — investors and journalists. People with lots of money, and people who find things out for a living."

He laughed. "So you think any secrets will quickly be uncovered."

"No doubt," she said. "No doubt whatsoever."

"Well, I just wanted to ask you to look after his physical safety while he's there. The conference is at a time we are out of session, so being gone from here won't be an issue, and I'll cover your travel and ... other ... costs."

"Where's the conference?"

"Mérida."

"I could stand some time there, I'm sure. Oh, and I have a partner ... we work together."

The unspoken question hung for just a moment, and Dr. Sorenson shrugged his shoulders. "Sure. That's fine."

"What about after the conference? Will he be coming back here? Will the people you're worried about follow him here?"

Dr. Sorenson had obviously not considered that possibility. He looked at her, then stared out the window, then shook his head. "I guess I can't do anything about that. I just want to add a little extra assurance that he makes it through the conference, I guess.

After that ..." He shrugged again. "What will be, will be."

"Very well. I'll need this much to start ..." She wrote on a post-it and handed it to him. "Make it out to me personally, and when it clears, we're in business. That much again will be due after the conference. Plus expenses."

He stared at the piece of paper, and she waited. He nodded, looked up, and said, "All right." He opened a computer bag and handed her a brochure from El Destino Resort Spa and Casino. "I'll have two rooms reserved for you the night the conference begins through the night after it ends."

"Here," she said, writing on a notepad. "Put them in these names."

"Really?"

She smiled and said nothing.

He stood up. She did the same. "And our job," she said, "is to keep him alive and get him on the plane back home. Is that it?"

He nodded. "I'd consider that a job satisfactorily completed. Actually, I don't know his travel plans, so I don't know if he's coming back here. Let's just say 'on the plane'."

They shook hands, and Dr. Sorenson left. Jennie closed the door behind him. She went to a filing cabinet, pulled out a folder named 'Personal', and sat down at her desk. A moment later she was opening a letter from Celena with a Venezuelan postmark.

# Chapter 18

Leonard sliced the end off the forbidden Cuban cigar and lifted a lighter to it as the door opened with a polite knock. He took a deep pull on it and blew great cumulus clouds of smoke into the sky above his desk. They drifted up into the chandelier and towards the upper level windows.

"Boss?"

"Yeah, been waiting for you. Do you know anything about this guy?"

"He's a college kid, in his last year. From upstate New York, around the lake country. Nothin' on him in the usual places. Google never heard of him. And the conference is bein' put on by somebody I never heard of. I think it's not his real name."

"The sponsor, or the guy talkin'?"

"The sponsor. Nothing checks out, about him."

"So it could be one of our friends, running a scam. Paying the hotel in cash. Figures."

"So, you wanna go?"

"Mérida? Of course I want to go, schmuck. Business expense, deductible."

"Assuming you ever pay any taxes?"

"Yeah, assuming that."

"Shall we just lift him from there and bring him back here after he talks?"

"You mean, without his permission and all? That would be kidnapping, wouldn't it?" Leonard put on his best expression of shock and dismay.

"Yeah, boss, I think that's what they call it. But I was just gonna call it a follow-up meeting, or, what's that fancy word for makin' people tell you what they know? 'Debriefing', that's what I like. You wanna debrief him?"

"We got extra bedrooms here, yeah, let's invite him up if what he says looks interesting. We'll offer him enough that he'll come on his own... and if he won't take it, then we'll know he's a fake."

"So, just you and me?"

"Yeah, sign me up for the conference, but use a fake name for you. And just hang around in the hotel, don't bother going to the meetings."

"Uh, boss, one other thing?"

"Yeah? Talk to me." He tried to blow a smoke ring, but it scrambled immediately.

"That girl Jennie, the journalist? She's registered. Fake name, same as before. I stole the list."

Leonard scowled. "I hate her, you know that, right?"

Yes, he knew that.

"We know where she lives, right?"

Yes, he knew where she lived.

"Get rid of her. She'll blow my cover, if she's there. Just take her out. When she gets in the car to head for the airport, take her out. And you do it personally, nobody else, just go do it, I don't care how. Push her into that lake, whatever. And don't tell me what happens, just bump her off and then catch your plane to meet me there."

"Got it."

When the man left, Leonard had second thoughts. Might take more than the schmuck, to get the job done. Might need to send someone else. Just in case. He picked up the phone.

“What do you want for your birthday, honey, and what calibre does it shoot?”

He smiled at her. “You choose, babe. Something to make our life complete.”

She leaned back toward the computer, and eased the mouse forward so the cursor floated over “Check Out.”

“Done. Let’s find dinner.”

The rifle arrived as they finished packing, just in time to be tucked into checked baggage. It disassembled into parts that would X-ray as household items, nothing suspicious. A toothbrush, a set of screwdrivers, some specialty wrenches, an odd-looking tube that would be transparent on the screen. An unusual bottle opener, but obviously just that. Nothing more.

“You shipped cartridges to the hotel?”

She nodded. “We certainly couldn’t pack them ... that might be a clue!”

“Yeah, even the TSA might pick that one up.”

“Unlikely.” She looked over the open suitcases. Racquets, swim suits and goggles, all the expected vacation items. Holsters of velcro and nylon, disassembled to not be obvious.

“Think we’re expected?” he asked, opening the blinds on the front window.

She came to his side. A quiet street, with the neighbors mostly at work. A small black sedan in the shade of an oak in the next block.

Maybe, she thought. Maybe we are. Hope not.

Mac closed the blinds, snapped the suitcases closed and jerked them off the bed. “We gotta pack lighter, honey! I’m getting too old for this!”

She laughed at him, trotted down the stairs and pulled the front door open. “Go be obvious, OK? Slam some car doors. Make sure everyone knows I’m leaving!”

He strode outside to the driveway, started raising the garage door and shouted, “Jennie, where’s that other brown suitcase? Are you taking it too?"

That should do it, she thought. That should do it!

Jennie pushed the brown suitcase into the back seat of the 4Runner, stepped back from the car, and waved to the house.

"Bye, honey. See you in a few weeks!"

Surely everyone in the neighborhood heard that.

She eased into the driver's seat and pulled the seat belts tight. The black car still lurked a block away. Couldn't tell from here if it was occupied, but she'd bet a new Ektelon racquet that it was.

Got everything? She looked in the glove compartment and nodded. She dug the small red tube out of her purse and set it between the seats, leaving the purse on the passenger seat.

No one coming? She backed out, turned north, and headed for the airport highway. Waiting at the traffic light, she saw nothing behind her until just as she pulled across traffic turning east. There it was, coming up to the light just soon enough to make it through. When it turned east behind her, there was no doubt.

Should have thrown a pair of nice New Balance shoes into the bargain!

The road wound past a shopping center, more neighborhoods, and then out into a long stretch of country road winding between rolling hills. Sure glad there's no kudzu. Those oaks and pines are beautiful, and that weed would cover them all.

The iron bridge took her high over Sentinel River, then down just above the water level and onto the long, flat concrete bridge over the lake. Somewhere in the middle she looked around. No one coming behind her but the black car, one other vehicle in the distance behind that, and the oncoming lanes across the divider were empty.

About ... about here, I think.

She wobbled the steering wheel quickly back and forth, then hit the brakes, coasting into the wide pavement shoulder and up close to the guardrails. Hot day, no wind. Be nice to get to the beach.

The black car cruised slowly up behind her and stopped. Jennie threw the door open, stepped out and walked quickly back, motioning to the driver to roll down his window.

Hope I look frantic enough.

She came to the side of the car and the heavily tinted window rolled slowly down. A roughly-shaven face turned towards her without expression.

"Can you help me?" she asked, as the window opened completely, raising her right hand to shield her eyes from the morning sun.

A black muzzle raised from the car interior and pointed at her chest. The man smiled.

She glanced at it. "Let me guess. Glock 21, .45 calibre? You wouldn't be caught with anything smaller."

The man reached up and pulled off his sunglasses, staring at her.

"I thought so," she said, as she squeezed the trigger in her left hand and unloaded the pepper spray into his face. Stepping aside to dodge the bullet fired by his convulsion, she grabbed the muzzle of the .45 and twisted it back against his thumb until he let it go.

"Sorry," she said, turning the canister and spraying the rest of whatever was in the car. "Just cayenne pepper, but quite tasty I'm sure." She walked back to her car, blowing out the black car's front tire and tossing the gun off the bridge as she went.

As she buckled the seat belt and drove away, she saw a black pickup truck pull in behind the black sedan.

Mac glided to a stop behind the black car and watched his wife drive away.

Be glad it wasn't me, he thought. She was probably kind.

He ran up to the car, pulled the XD from a waistband holster and fired a single shot through the side back window across whoever might be in the back seat. Looking through the driver's open window he saw no one in the passenger seat, and Jennie's new acquaintance was rubbing his face and screaming. Mac yanked open the door, dragged the incapacitated man out and threw him to the pavement.

No seatbelt, he thought. Typical.

He reached in past the steering wheel, pulled the keys out of the ignition, and popped open the trunk.

The man struggled to his feet, trying to see through the chemical pain and find out who was there. Mac pulled him towards the back of the car, slipped the man's wallet out of the left inside coat pocket, and shoved him backwards into the trunk. A moment later he had the feet tucked in as well and slammed the trunk shut. Tossing the keys into the lake below them, he trotted back to the F150 and settled in.

Browsing through the wallet, he removed a few hundred dollars and a driver's license.

"Well, well, well. We meet again." He threw it into gear. About a mile down the road he slowed down, put the passenger window down, and tossed the wallet where the water moccasins could munch on what was left of their cousin's paperwork.

Nasty business, he thought. Why can't people just get along?

# Chapter 19

Jennie circled up to the 5th level in parking garage C, nosed into a spot in the corner looking out over the runways, and noted the time. A Delta commuter flight lifted off and gracefully tilted left, heading into the sun.

Mac wants to fly some places. Maybe we can do that. Never too old, right? Just need to put a little cash away, and make the time.

She opened the door at exactly eight minutes past the hour, stepped out, and looked around. No one in sight, except the couple with the stroller just coming out of the elevator. She hoisted the brown bag, dropped it onto its rollers, and walked slowly to the elevators.

Coming out on the ticketing floor, she scanned the crowds moving through the corridors. After all these years, it was habit to scan the crowd, looking for ... whatever. Everyone looked normal. Falling in line, she moved up to the Elite check-in counter and pushed the bag up on the scale.

"Good morning, ma'am," said the blue uniform with the Australian accent. "One bag?"

"Yes, thanks." She handed him her pre-printed boarding pass, and watched the scale readout. Forty-nine pounds. She smiled.

"Just under, ma'am. You're good to go. Here's your boarding pass with the bag ticket."

The bag went on the conveyer belt with a thud, and she loitered long enough to see it disappear behind the rubber flaps.

Behave yourself, she thought, watching it go. Don't attract any attention! You're just a normal brown suitcase, so act like it!

The line was still short at the security checkpoint. She slipped off her shoes, dropped them and her purse into a bucket, and set the iPad into another one. The gangly fellow lounging at the entrance to the scanners eyed her belongings.

"No carry-on?"

"I travel light."

He smirked and motioned her into the scanner, still looking at that iPad.

"Feet on the marks, please," said the next agent, "hands over your head." The scanner whirled past. "This way."

As she waited for clearance, the agent put his hand on her back. "Just sweat. Looks solid on the scan."

"You do know you just violated the Fourth Amendment, right?"

"Huh? You causing trouble?"

She paused in the main corridor, looking for coffee. A city policeman strolled by.

"Excuse me, officer?"

"Yes, ma'am?" he said, stopping to look at her carefully.

"You know what they're doing back there is not legal, right? The part about searches without a warrant? And this is your city?"

"Sorry, ma'am, that's federal property across that line, and they do whatever they want." He strolled on.

Exactly the problem, she thought. And he's probably been told it's perfectly fine.

The green and white Starbucks sign glowed brightly just past the security area, and she headed that way, pulling a credit card from her wallet as she tucked the boarding pass inside. A handsome man with a little too much wear and tear for his 50 years stepped into line behind her and cleared his throat.

"Excuse me, ma'am, did you drop this?" He offered her a folded up dollar bill.

"Why, yes... thanks." She took it, slipped into the wallet, and extended her hand. "I'm Clara. You are?"

"Hank, ma'am. Pleased to make your acquaintance."

"Have we met before?"

"Reckon not, ma'am. I'd surely remember." He smiled awkwardly.

"May I help you?" The barista was ready.

"Chai tea latte, please, with vanilla and Splenda."

Hank stepped up beside her. "Here, let me get this. Straight coffee for me, miss, none of that foo-foo in it, thank you. And I'll get the lady's drink too."

"Thank you, Hank! Nice to meet a gentleman."

"My pleasure, ma'am. Where might you be headed today?"

"Mérida."

"Ahh," he smiled.

"No, it's mainly work. Got a conference to attend."

"Me, too! You going to that investor thing, that guy with the software?"

"Why, yes. You're going there?"

"I am. Got a little to invest, kinda like to see what he has to say. And I like the cigars they get for you at El Destino. That where you're stayin' too?"

"Veinte chai, coffee!"

"Here, our drinks are ready. You going on Jazz Air, the 3:00 flight?"

"The same."

"Well, I'll be. Let's wander that way, ain't got a whole lotta time. What brings you to the conference?"

"Reporter. Freelance writer, really, on assignment for some financial rags on the coast. Can't let the Wall Street Journal have all the headlines!"

"So when you figure out what he's sayin', you can explain it to the rest of us. Good. I like that."

He touched the rim of his hat. "Appreciate it!"

Mac strolled along beside "Clara" and watched the crowds waiting in the gate lobbies.

"What's our gate?"

"I think it's 35, Hank. We're almost there. Do you fly much?"

"Not so much, ma'am, not so much. Kind of a homebody." A man in front of 34 slouched in his chair by the window and pretended to read a paper. Mac pretended not to see him, just to play fair. His clothes were a little too fine, his choice of paper a little too wrong, and his lack of any carry-on bag was unusual.

Popeye, thought Mac. I'll call him Popeye.

They stood in the middle of the concourse, chatting as though strangers, until the flight was called. Popeye had wandered up and waited a few feet behind them. Six foot even, trim, very balanced, broad in the shoulders, fidgety in the eyes.

"Traveling with anyone, ma'am?" asked Mac.

"Clara" glanced at Popeye. "No, I'm by myself. Just another day at work."

"First class, active duty service, anyone needing extra time to board, you are welcome to board at this time ... Elite customers are welcome to board through this line, over the red carpet, at your convenience. Boarding by row number will begin shortly."

Popeye stepped past them and walked quickly onto the plane. When their rows were called, Mac and Jennie boarded, entering with a few people between them in the line. Popeye sat in the front of the plane and studied them as they walked past him down the aisle. Mac stepped into aisle 12 and pushed his bag into the overhead compartment. He stood facing back until Jennie reached her seat in 17 and settled in by the window. She waved at him, and he nodded and took his seat.

Popeye was gone by the time they filed up through first class and out of the plane. Mac walked down the corridor, following the baggage claim signs, and found the carousel with the Jazz Air sign. His bag came along soon, and he rolled it out to the taxi stand.

"Oh, Mr. Hank..." came the voice from behind him. He turned.

"Why, howdy, miss ... Clara, was it?"

"Yes, how good of you to remember. If you're getting a taxi, perhaps we could share a ride. I believe you said something about the Destino?"

"Certainly, ma'am, be glad to. I am going there, you're right as rain."

"Next!" called the porter, and cab 2292 rolled up. The driver threw their bags into the trunk and opened the door on his side for Jennie. Mac went around and climbed into the other side.

"El Destino, please?"

The meter clicked on and immediately showed $2.40. "My goodness," said Jennie, "you're making several hundred dollars per hour!" The cabbie laughed, "It's not four miles away, ma'am, I got to make it however I can!"

In minutes they were at the hotel, and he set their suitcases on the ground.

Mac handed him fifty dollars. "Got a card? I may need you in a hurry sometime."

The cabbie looked at the fifty dollar bill and dug out a card. "Anytime, Mister, day or night, I'm your man. Here's my cell phone." He pointed to the card. "Just ask for Andy, and say it's 'Cowboy' callin', and I'll jump right to it!"

"Thanks, my friend."

"You oughta get to know this man," said the cabbie to Jennie. "He looks like a right nice fella!"

"Think so?" She looked Mac up and down. "You really think so?"

Andy waved at her and climbed back in taxi. "Make up your own mind, missy, but I'm thinkin' he's a good one!"

"Me, too," whispered Jennie, and winked at Mac. "Me, too."

# Chapter 20

"Name, please?"

"Clara. Clara Watson."

The clerk tapped on the keyboard, and the printer responded. "Here for the financial conference? This is the schedule, with a map of the rooms being used. It's a big place," he smiled at her. "And your room keys. One, or more?"

"Better give me two. I always lose one."

"Certainly." He handed her a small envelope. "The network key is written inside. Complimentary, of course. Breakfast from 6 to 10, just over there, behind you, in the restaurant."

She took the envelope and information packet, and stepped away. "Hank" was next.

"Williams. Hank Williams."

The clerk looked up at him. "Hank" touched a finger to the brim of his cowboy hat, and never cracked a smile.

"Thank you, Mr. ... Williams."

He took his package and turned to see "Clara" in the middle of the lobby, looking around.

"Miss ... um, Watson, is it?"

"Why, yes, Mr. ... Williams?"

"Yes, that's right. Are you free for dinner? I believe the first event is not until tomorrow."

"I am, actually. Meet you over there?" she pointed at the restaurant entrance, "In about half an hour? The 'Brizas del Mar?'"

"Certainly."

They walked together to the elevator. Jennie held her room key envelope so he could see the room number, and handed him her extra key. He did the same for her.

“Do you sing, Hank?”

They stepped into the elevator, alone together for the first time all day. He pressed the buttons for their floors, turned, and wrapped her up in his arms. “Only when I’m with you. My room is on a higher floor. Want to share the view?”

“Why, Mr. Williams, how nice of you. Yes. Shall I meet you there now, or later?”

The elevator chimed as it reached her floor, and they stood apart as strangers would. The door opened and closed. They looked at each other.

“How about now?”

“I have at least half an hour before my next appointment.”

“Really! Hmm, so do I.”

"Front desk? This is Williams, in 622... oh, I guess you can see that, can't you. Have you got a package for me? Should have come in a couple of days ago. Small, but kinda heavy."

He looked over at Jennie pouring drinks in the kitchen area, and nodded.

"Just have someone bring it up, would you? Thanks."

He hung up and Jennie brought the glasses to the coffee table.

Mac tossed his suitcase onto the bed and popped open the latches. He lifted out the tube and fished around for the related parts.

"Did TSA open it, by the way?"

Mac looked at the combination lock on the suitcase. "Nope... at least, the color indicator didn't change."

"I am so not surprised."

"Jennie, they would not have known what they were looking at, if they took every bit of this and laid it on a table."

She smiled. "Got all the pieces?"

"Wish we'd had time to test it out." He assembled the muzzle, the stock, the trigger mechanism, and the sights. "7.62, right?"

"That's what I ordered."

Someone knocked at the door, and Jennie stepped out of sight. Mac placed the rifle under the bedspread and went to the door.

"Your package, sir? Just sign here."

"How much did you get?" he asked, closing the door behind him. "Feels like more than 50 rounds."

"Couple hundred. Think that's enough?"

"With that and what I've got for the XD, I think we have enough!" he laughed. "Maybe our friend from the taxi can take me someplace to try it out."

Popeye watched her emerge from the elevator, look around, and wander towards the restaurant. She sat down where she was looking out over the lobby and gaming tables, and her eyes slowly swept the room, her line of sight passing over him without pausing.

She's a cool one. Is she really a journalist, or something else? How can I get her away from that jerk cowboy?

He stayed immobile, waiting. Four minutes, five minutes. The elevator opened again and Cowboy came out, western shirt pressed smooth and boots shining. Popeye hated him already.

Did he look at me? Did he recognize me? Popeye casually looked away.

The cowboy smoothed his hair and walked quickly to the restaurant, waving to Clara. She stood to meet him. Popeye could just hear their conversation, and resisted the urge to turn towards them and listen more intently.

"Mr. Williams, you remembered."

"Well, of course. Clara? May I call you Clara?"

"Certainly... Hank."

"Shall we?"

Their conversation drifted out of earshot, as they entered the restaurant.

Hank? Hank Williams? Is this a joke? A nickname? Country hick parents? He shook his head, and noticed the time. Give it ten minutes, then drift in and get a seat near them. Meantime... a few pulls on the slot machine won't hurt anything.

Ten minutes later he cursed, watched his last quarter disappear, and turned to the restaurant just in time to hear Philip Cross introduce himself to the clerk at the service counter. Popeye looked at a newspaper for a minute, then strolled to the elevator and pushed the "up" button when Philip turned away from the clerk and began walking to the elevators.

Popeye turned away from the elevator buttons, looked at Philip approaching, and said, "Going up?"

"Yeah. Yeah, I am."

"Aren't you that financial software guy?"

Philip looked at him sharply. "Yes. Are you coming to the conference?"

"Haven't registered. Is it too late?"

They stepped in and the elevator doors closed. "Floor?" said Popeye.

"Two. Thanks."

"Oh. Me, too. So, can I still register?"

"I suppose so. Somebody else manages that, of course."

"Yeah, of course. When do you start?"

"Tomorrow morning. 9 am."

The door opened on 2. "Will you excuse me?" Philip rushed out and turned left.

"Sure, sure, thanks." Popeye stepped out and followed slowly. Philip turned the corner; Popeye hurried to the corner and walked slowly around it. Philip fumbled for his room key halfway down on the left, and Popeye gave him plenty of time to get in and close the door before meandering past.

Got it. Good to know.

He turned on his heel and got back to the elevator, disappearing into one heading down before Philip returned.

In the lobby, he strolled into the restaurant and noticed where Clara and the cowboy were seated. "Over there by the window, in the corner?" he asked the greeter, and she led him to that table, about three back from his target. "Thanks. Coffee. Black."

The waitress brought plates to Clara's table. Clara faced Popeye, shielded partly by the cowboy. He could hear her perfectly.

"I always enjoyed the Popeye cartoons, didn't you?"

What was that about? 'Popeye'? Good grief.

"One of my favorites," agreed Cowboy. "Seen any recently?"

"Yes, in fact, set in some resort area. Pretty amusing."

This is ridiculous.

# Chapter 21

Leonard climbed into a cab at the Mérida airport.

"El Destino," he muttered, and pulled a cigar from his bag.

"Yes, sir," said Andy, and reached a lighter back. "Coming for that financial meeting?"

"Shut up," said Leonard, after lighting his cigar.

Halfway to the hotel Leonard broke the silence. "You seen a lady coming to this meeting? Short blonde hair, maybe 30 or so, good-lookin', athletic?"

"No sir, and I would remember."

"If you see her, call me. Just ask for Leonard at the hotel." He tossed a silver dollar to the front seat.

They stopped in front of the Resort and Andy came around to open his door. He did not bother to offer a tip as Andy handed him his suitcase and he marched up the steps. Tips were for extra help, and this guy was just being a regular cabbie.

Leonard looked carefully around the lobby as he strolled in. Didn't see her. Didn't see Schmuck either.

He looked over the clerk at the counter as she waited to help him.

"Your name?"

"Yeah... Leonard. You look nice."

"Is that your ... last name?"

"Just look it up, you'll find me."

"Apparently you're the only person named Leonard in the system today. Found you just fine. From Chicago?"

"Yeah. Two keys, and send up some Scotch. And if someone calls for Leonard, you know where to send it."

"Yes, sir, and the Scotch is in the room waiting for you.

Anything else?"

"Maybe," he smiled, and turned away. The elevators were fast, and he was on the top floor.

Nice to have people who do what you say.

The key worked on the first swipe, and the air conditioning was set correctly. He pulled the glass door open, stepped out onto the balcony, and looked down at the lounge chairs around the pool. "Stupid," he muttered, "just get burned out there."

Then he remembered a time in his life when he would have been down there all day, and cursed. Getting old. Getting fat. Getting sloppy.

Yeah, so what? Shut up.

He returned to the air conditioning, opened the bottle, poured half a glass, and downed it. Where's the schmuck? What if something went wrong? May need Plan B. He placed a couple of local calls and got who he wanted.

"Ramón?"

"Quién es?"

"Leonard. Get two guys over to the Destino. Now. 901."

OK, now. What about this Cross guy?

He picked up the room phone.

"Cross, please."

"Excuse me?" came the reply.

"Connect me to Mr. Cross. Don't know his room."

"Yes, sir. 217." In a moment the phone rang.

"Hello?"

"Cross?"

"Uh... yes?"

"You got time to talk? I'm on 9. First suite to the right."

"No, I really don't ... I'm getting ready for the meeting. But who is this?"

"Leonard. Chicago. You'll be coming to my place after this is over."

"I don't think so, actually. I have other plans."

"You had other plans. No problem. Just a day or two, maybe more. We'll have fun."

He smiled, and listened to the silence on the other end.

"But I'm busy ... Leonard ... I need to go."

"That's fine. I'll expect you in five minutes. 901." And he hung up.

Sounds like the schmuck didn't make the ... arrangements. Not here yet, I guess. He sat down and waited. Cross would come up. No one ever refused Leonard.

The tap on the door came right on schedule.

Mac decided he needed to get out. Let Jennie prepare for the meetings, he couldn't endure any more idle time!

Where was that cabbie's name ... ah, here it is. Andy. And he called me 'Cowboy.'

"Hey, Andy, it's me, 'Cowboy' callin'. Is Cab 2292 busy this afternoon?"

"Mr. Cowboy, sir, yes sir, I am, I got a full afternoon booked with a Mr. Cowboy at the Destino!"

"That sounds like a great idea. But I need a special favor... you need to help me disappear."

"Mr. Cowboy, sir, I can do that. I am your man. But you know the town is only four frog hops wide, and everybody knows everybody. So disappearing is a pretty good trick."

"I knew you were the man who could do it. Come on!"

"On my way, Mr. Cowboy, sir!"

The taxi came screeching up, the passenger door flew open, and everyone in sight was watching.

Mac strolled out and stood at the curb until Andy got out and came around.

"Now, Andy. How am I going to disappear," he asked quietly, "if you come in like an F-16 blowing up terrorist camps, and everyone in Mérida is watching me get in your cab?"

"Oh, sorry, Mr. Cowboy, sir, but the disappearin' part is what happens next. I had no idea you needed to disappear while you were actually standin' in front of the hotel itself!"

Mac laughed. "That's fine, gives them all something to talk about. Here, toss this in the back for me." He handed Andy a dark blue gym bag and slid into the passenger seat. Andy stored the bag somewhere and jumped into the driver's seat. The cab pulled away slowly and with great apparent caution.

"Much better, thank you."

They drove out onto the Avenida and turned south. "Where you be wantin' to be invisible at, Mr. Cowboy?"

Mac slipped his wallet out of his jacket pocket, opened it, and handed Andy a hundred dollar bill. "I'd like to test a new rifle, and when I'm finished, I'd like for no one on earth to know I have it."

Andy looked over at him with raised eyebrows, took the bill, and smiled. "Did and done. Out the west side of town. Got me a place there, ain't nobody around. Tourists ain't found it yet!"

Mac rolled the window down and dug some sunglasses out of his jacket pocket, as Andy spun the car around and took a smaller road. He picked up a copy of Mérida Today from the dashboard. "Nice day to not be found!"

"Indeed it is, Mr. Cowboy, sir. What kind of gun are we testin' today?"

"Oh, just a small rifle. The kind they let you put in the carry-on bag, when you catch the plane."

"Now, Mr. Cowboy, sir, now you are pullin' my leg for sure. There ain't no kind of rifle they let you put on the carry-on no more."

"Used to be. You remember?"

"Yes, oh sure I do. I ain't no baby chicken, been around a while. Used to carry rifles up there when goin' huntin', whatever. And never had no terrorists, either."

"You been in the army, Andy? Know how to shoot?"

"I can drop a blossom off a cactus at a hundred meters, yessir.

And a boa at fifty, while he's a runnin'."

"You've got boa constrictors here?"

"Big ones. But we don't have a boa problem, Mr. Cowboy... the boas have an Andy problem!"

Mac laughed. "Well, my rifle shoots a 7.62 shell. Ever heard of it?"

"Yes, sir, Mr. Cowboy, it's a popular size these days. Be a great one for the boas!"

"Got any other varmints around? Any of the two-legged kind?"

"Afraid so, Mr. Cowboy. Got some locals, and I know most of 'em, and the outsiders they mostly hire the locals. Are we bein' invisible because of them?"

"That's a fair guess, though I don't know who. How far to your place?"

Thirty minutes later they were standing on desert ground a thousand yards from any road, surrounded by scrub brush and scattered cactus plants. The cab was tucked into a low gully, well out of sight from anyone passing by.

"There's some cactus that could use some trimmin'," said Andy, pointing to a clump of them to the north. "And I'm guessing you can tell where you hit them by the hole you're gonna leave."

"Maybe so. Let's try it out."

Mac opened the gym bag and began assembling the rifle. Andy watched from a few feet away.

"How did you get that here, Mr. Cowboy? TSA let it go through?"

"You can pack them in luggage, if you fill out the forms. But then everyone knows about it. They don't really know what to look for, if it's in pieces like this. And I wanted this one to be off the radar."

Andy nodded, and stepped a little closer. "No safety. No scope. This won't be a hunting rifle, will it, sir?"

"No, you're right. It's a bit more serious than hunting." Mac raised the stock to his shoulder and fired, in a single motion. A small black hole appeared in the center of a cactus pad fifty yards away.

"Nice. Can you stack one on top of it, sir?"

A second hole appeared six inches above the first one.

"Very nice, Mr. Cowboy, sir. Would you be wanting me to keep an eye on some of them varmints we were discussin'?"

"That could be a very good thing, Andy. Tell you what. If we need some help, and things proceed to a good conclusion, I'd be willing to leave this rifle with you as compensation. What do you think?"

"Since I can't get one here any way legal, Mr. Cowboy, I'd be grateful. And I suppose you'd rather leave it than try to fool the TSA twice?"

"They might be awake next time, you're right. Want to give it a try?"

"Sure, Mr. Cowboy, sir. I'll put me a new hole right above those two."

And he did. Then he turned quickly, aimed at the ground some twenty yards away, and fired once more. A long reptile jerked into the air, thrashed around in the sand and rocks, and lay still.

"Well done, Andy. I had just noticed him myself. Friend of yours?"

"Used to be. Stealin' my chickens, that's the crime. Reckon we're even."

"Reckon you are! But I think you're a little more even than he is!"

"I believe I've met one of your friends, Mr. Cowboy. Brought him to the hotel same day you came. Big guy, ugly, smokes a Cuban. Habano, I think, maybe a Montecristo number 4, smelled like it."

"Is there anything you don't know about, Andy?"

"Ice cream." He looked at Mac for a moment, and finally cracked a smile. "Really. Don't know anything about it!"

"Anything else about my friend? Say what he's here for?"

"Oh, sure, everyone talks. Here for that financial thing. Asked me about a lady, in fact, if I had seen her, and pretty well drew me a picture of that lady you rode with. Like he knew her, and was real nervous about if she had come."

"What did you tell him?"

"Told him I ain't never seen anyone like that, and I would have remembered. That's what I told him. Paid me to call him, if I saw her."

"Well, he'll find her soon enough. Thanks, Andy. I'll tell her you covered for her."

"Sure thing, Mr. Cowboy. You ready to go back?"

# Chapter 22

"Yeah, come in. Scotch on the table. Sit there."

Philip Cross stepped into the room and stared. He had never drunk Scotch, never been in a luxury suite, and never been manipulated so easily as by this man.

He walked past the drink and sat down, straight up on the front of the chair. "Who are you?"

The man smiled. "Does your stuff work?"

He hesitated. "Who are you?"

"Son," said Leonard, "I told you. I'm Leonard. Chicago. Do I have to tell you everything twice?"

Philip shook his head. "What do you want? I'm busy."

"You want money, right?"

Philip nodded.

"I have money. You have software. I want software. You have software and you want money... I have money and I want software. Got it, or do I need to go slower?"

Philip sat back in the chair and examined Leonard, who sliced and lit a cigar while he waited for an answer. Suddenly a sense of deja-vu came over Philip, and he tried to remember where he had seen this man before... but no such nightmare came to mind.

"I got it. Now what?"

"How much do you want for your stuff?"

"Depends on my partner."

"He didn't tell you? He sent you here to pitch it, and didn't tell you what to do when some big fish bites on the bait?"

Philip reached into his shirt pocket and pulled out a business card with two items on it: the name "Doc" and a phone number. He handed it to Leonard.

Leonard picked up the hotel phone, put it on the speaker, and dialed the number.

"Yes?"

"Is this 'Doc'?"

"Yes."

"This is Leonard. From Chicago. I have your boy in my room. How much do you want for the stuff?"

"What do you mean, 'you have him'?"

"Relax, Doc, he's just visiting. I invited him up for a chat. How much do you want?"

"Exclusive?"

"Of course."

"A million."

"I'll give you 600 grand, and another 400 when I see it works. Cash."

Silence. Then, over the speaker, "Phil, are you OK?"

"Yeah, fine."

"You good with that?"

"Don't know anything about him ... 'Doc'."

"Yeah, I got that. But let's do it."

"OK."

"Leonard, here's the routing info. You ready?"

Leonard picked up the hotel notepad and pen. "Go."

When the numbers were given and repeated, Leonard added a condition. "Here's the deal, Doc, or whatever your name is. I'm going to send this money, and then Philip and I are going to get on a plane to my place for a private screening. Here's the phone number."

He rattled off the number. "Got it?"

"Yeah, I got it, but ..."

"No 'but'. I just told you how this is going down. When I see it works, I'll send him home and you get the rest of the money. If I see it doesn't work, I'll come looking for my 600 big ones." And he hung up.

Philip stood up. "What do you mean, 'your place'? I've got a presentation to do!"

"Sit down, Cross. You just sold the goods. You got no meeting. I'm your meeting. We're gonna gather up your stuff and hit the road."

A knock, a single knock, sounded at the door.

"Come in," yelled Leonard. Two men walked in. Locals, by their look.

"You Leonard?" said one, with a glance at Philip.

"Yeah."

"Ramón sent us."

Leonard nodded. "Good. Take this young man back to his room — 217, I believe — and gather up his stuff. All of it. Scrub the room. Take him to the United check-in counter at the airport at exactly ... nine o'clock tonight. If he's been drinking a little by then, so I need to help him onto the plane, well, that'll be just fine. But I don't think he will."

"Right, Mr. Cross? We have a deal? I send the money, and you come with me. Right?"

Philip looked at all the men around him - tough, serious, ugly men - and nodded.

"Fine. Now give the gentlemen your room key, so we don't have any difficulties. They'll wait with you while you pack. And don't worry about the meeting... I'll cancel it for you. Oh, and do you have a cell phone? Let me have it. You won't need it while you're with ... us."

He walked over to the glass door, still open to the balcony, and stepped out to the railing. "Look, Mr. Cross, there's a swimming pool. Wonder if I can reach it from here ..."

Looking back with a smile, he tossed Phillip's phone high in the air.

Jennie sat in the front row, off to the side where she could keep an eye on the double doors leading into the presentation room. She sipped the chai tea latte and wished there had been more on the breakfast buffet. Glancing back, she saw Mac wander in, slip off his western hat and settle into the back corner of the room. Always cautious, always observant. He winked at her across the crowd.

The meeting should have started thirty minutes ago. People talked, fussed, complained. A stooped elderly gentleman stood up at the other end of the front row and spoke to the crowd, or anyone in it who happened to notice he was speaking.

"What's going on? Anybody know?"

Murmurs of complaint and frustration welled up, but apparently no one knew.

A hotel manager came in and walked to the podium. He tapped on the microphone, and slowly the room turned its attention to him.

"Has anyone seen Mr. Cross?" he asked. Silence. Jennie looked back just in time to see Mac disappear through the doors.

"What do you mean?" shouted someone in the middle of the crowd. "Isn't he checked in?"

"Yes," nodded the manager, "but there's no answer at his door, and the 'do not disturb' sign is on the handle. I thought perhaps someone had seen him this morning, at breakfast perhaps."

Apparently no one had. People began standing up and looking about.

Jennie slipped down the aisle and out of the room, jumped into the stairwell, trotted up one flight, and almost ran to room 217. As she turned the corner, she saw Mac closing the door behind him and peeling off the latex gloves.

"Andy's on the way; let's go for a scenic ride together. Cross is gone."

"Right," she said, and suddenly they became two strangers walking different ways in the hallway. She went down the far stairway while Mac strolled back to the elevator.

Jennie walked up to Mac in the milling crowd in front of the hotel entrance. "Mr. Williams, I was thinking of taking a ride around the city. Would you join me?"

"Absolutely," he said, and waved for a cab. "Great idea. Nothing else to do now, since the meeting is apparently delayed a bit..."

He stepped across the lane of taxis waiting for passengers as Andy's cab arrived and pulled into another lane. The taxi manager waved them back. Mac stepped over to him, shook hands, and spoke quietly. The man looked at his hand, patted Mac on the shoulder, and sent him on his way. Jennie followed, as Andy walked around the cab and opened the door.

"He won't bother you," said Mac, and Andy nodded. They settled into the back seat.

"Andy. Cross has disappeared. Any idea what happened?"

"Yes, Mr. Cowboy, sir. Heard some of the local guys were at the hotel last night to hustle someone to the airport. Could be your guy?"

"When?"

"Late. Maybe for that United flight that leaves at 10?"

"Let's find out."

They pulled out into traffic and turned towards the airport.

Jennie dug her cell phone out and dialed a call.

"Dr. Sorenson?" Mac could not hear the response.

"I'm in Mérida. Where is he?" Again, he could not hear what was said.

She hung up. "Chicago."

Andy slammed on the brakes and slid over to the curb. Three cars surrounded them, pulling in close in front, behind, and on the street side. Men appeared on both sides of the car. Andy's hands did not leave the steering wheel. Mac's door was pulled open, hands reached in, and he was yanked out of the cab. He pushed one man away with a punch to the chest, twisted another man's arm up to force him to the ground, and the barrel of a shotgun was shoved into his stomach.

"No más."

# Chapter 23

The cars were gone as quickly as they came, and so was Mac.

"Andy, who are those people?"

"I don't know, Miss Clara. The one out here in the street, he pointed a gun at me, so I don't move. They're not from here, I don't think. But I got a license from the one in front of us. I can find out for you."

She pulled out a card and handed it to him. "Here's my number. In case you have to call me, now that Mr. Cowboy isn't here! And give me one of yours."

"Miss Clara, your name's not Miss Clara?"

"To everyone else here, it is. Is your name 'Andy'?

"Yes, ma'am, it is, except to my wife. And I can't tell you what she calls me!"

They both laughed.

"Thanks, Andy. I needed that. Now take me back to the hotel, please. I have to get our things before we go look for him."

When he pulled up to the curb at the hotel, Andy stopped her from getting out.

"Come stay with us."

She looked at him. "I should not stay here, for sure. Do you mean, at your house?"

"Yes. Come to our house. Maria knows about you and Mr. Cowboy. You'll be safe."

She opened Mac's room on the sixth floor and quickly slipped in. Nothing seemed out of place. His suitcase was on the extra bed, and everything was in it. Always ready to go, she thought. No packing needed. A real pro. But where's the rifle bag?

She looked into the bathroom, and a hand slapped over her mouth. An arm reached around her waist. She bit the hand at her mouth, and stomped down across the shin of whoever was behind her. Those two things broke him loose enough for her to grab the hand at her mouth, twist the fingers back to the point of breaking, and push that hand back away from her. The man staggered back. She twisted around, threw a straight hand edge into his throat, and kicked his knee straight in. It cracked, and he fell backwards onto the bed with a cry of pain. Popeye.

Anyone else? She looked around. The room seemed empty. The man struggled to get up on the other leg, and was fishing inside his waistband.

Great, now he's going to shoot me.

She grabbed the lamp from beside the bed, jerked it free from the socket, and swung, doing her best imitation of Joe DiMaggio reaching for the center field fence.

Maybe he'll live, she thought. Maybe.

She soaked a washcloth in the sink and wiped down the broken lamp, hoping to remove any fingerprints.

He must have been in the closet.

She looked, and found the rifle bag on the closet floor. A minute later she had gathered her bathroom supplies and headed down to the fourth floor. Five more minutes and she was at the front desk.

"401 and 622 are out," she said, dropping room keys on the counter. "Oh, and there's a body in 622," she said. "And the lamp is broken."

The clerk stared at her.

"You might want to call an ambulance before housekeeping gets there, but ..." Jennie shrugged. "Your choice."

She walked out to the sidewalk at the other end of the hotel from the taxi line. Andy gunned his cab to come get her.

“Here you are, my friend. I think this is yours.”

She set the rifle bag on the back floorboard, and Andy put the suitcases into the trunk. She opened the front passenger door and climbed in.

“Maybe you can find the guys that took Mr. Cross; I think they work for that fellow in the desert that’s been stealing your chickens!”

“I will do it.”

"Now ... let's help Mr. Cowboy, if we can. We have a few days before Chicago figures out that the software doesn't work. Where do you think they took him?"

Three days later, they sat at the kitchen table as Maria scooped a second helping of huevos rancheros onto their plates.

"Andy, we've talked to every bartender, policeman, and drug dealer that would talk to us. He's not here. And nobody knows who took him."

He nodded. "Don't know where else to look."

"It's time. I have to go."

"To the airport?"

“Please. I've got to get to Chicago. They'll kill him if I don't."

“And Mr. Cowboy?”

“I'm thinking Mr. Cowboy will have to take care of himself until I get back, or until you can find him. Seems like he can do that.”

“I’m thinkin’ you’re right, Miss Clara. And I’m thinkin’ you can too ...!”

She filed out of the plane into O’Hare airport, fretting about how slow the whole de-boarding process was.

But now what?

She pulled the slip of notepaper from her purse. “Leonard,” and a number. A Chicago gangster, a kidnapped kid, software that was probably a scam, and maybe a day or two to yank both the kid and the professor out of the soup.

She strolled to the back of an empty gate lobby and dialed the cellphone.

"Maggie?"

"Yes, may I help you?"

"Jennie. From school."

"No! What a treat! Where are you?"

"Just walked into O'Hare. I need some help from someone who knows their way around the wind-blown city."

"I'm as wind-blown as they come. How about lunch?"

"Thought you would never ask! I'll go out through baggage claim - United - and look for you. Black pants, black blouse ... you know, the stealth journalist look!"

"On my way. 17 minutes ... plus elevator ... see you at 11:20!"

Maggie pulled up exactly on schedule, and tossed her purse into the back. "Come in here!"

"Thanks, Maggie. My treat. Any good Italian food in Chicago?"

"Your first visit, and YOUR treat? I don't think so! Yeah, my favorite — you won't believe their spumoni!"

"Ah, you remembered. Sounds great."

After coffee and talking about all the old friends they could remember, Jennie pushed her chair back. "Got a simple question for you. Who is this, and how do I find him?"

She pushed the note across the table. 'Leonard,' and a phone number.

"The only 'Leonard in Chicago' I can think of is not the kind of guy you'd take on a date!"

"Then that's probably him. Talk to me."

"Filthy rich, arrogant, lawless, apparently immune from prosecution... which means he's bribed everyone in sight. Like everyone else does here! Is that his cell phone?"

"No idea. It's the number he gave ... a friend ... to reach him."

"Well, if he's had it a while, it looks like a cell prefix. That code is used for all kinds of numbers now, but it was just for cellphones when it started. So ... I guess the question is, how do you find him without letting him know you've found him?"

"Wait a minute. Is this the "Leo" from ten years ago who had more prostitution houses than rats in a New York subway tunnel?"

"The same."

"I know him. Worse, he knows me. Worse, I probably just took down two of his thugs."

"Excuse me?"

"Umm ... side business ... kind of a hobby ... I'm not always a nice girl. Actually a family business," she winked. "I married into it."

Maggie sat back and looked intently at Jennie. "OK... I think I can buy that. So he knows you, and you're looking for him ... because he just did something to you?"

"Did something to a friend I'm looking after. Brought him here a bit unwillingly, I suspect."

"No surprise there. Whether your friend is still alive may be the question. Does he know you're "looking after" this person?"

"As far as I know ... not yet. He knows I was coming to hear the man talk, like he was. But ... no, I don't think so."

"You and Leonard went to the same meeting somewhere? Oh, my goodness, let me try to imagine what meeting would have brought you two together! No, I can't. Unless you've been a very bad girl, I can't think what it would be! Unless ... of course, money. You write about it, and he chases it. Ok, well, your friend is in the trap. We gotta get him out quick."

"We? Maggie, this is ... "

"Hey. I'm a Chicago kid. Got the bruises and the enemies to prove it. Black belt Aikido, did you know?"

"No! That did not come up in class, that I recall!"

"It wasn't on the exam," she laughed. "So. Where would he put your friend, is the question. He owns the Plaza, and it's in a part of town where no questions are asked. That's my bet. Shall we settle in somewhere and plan our moves?"

# Chapter 24

Maggie parked two blocks away, facing her black Protege back towards the freeway entrance. They slowly climbed out of the car. Trash blew by on the street. No one was in sight. The late afternoon sun had no trees to bless, no grass to grow, just concrete and dust to heat.

"Don't bring anything you care about," said Maggie, popping open the trunk and dropping her purse into it. Jennie waved; she had left it all in her hotel. She looked around. A drug deal was going down two blocks away; the participants drifted apart, and a police car cruised past them moments later.

"Ready?" Maggie was waiting. They walked slowly towards the Plaza. A single taxi cruised by them, looking. Maggie waved him off, and he drifted on to be the only taxi waiting in the yellow lane in front of the Plaza.

They stepped onto the sidewalk in front of the hotel.

"Two well-dressed girls in this part of town... should draw some attention. Project roughness. Don't look soft or uncertain, whatever you do. They'll think we're a couple of street girls, if we do it right."

A bellhop lounged against the marble wall, idly kicking at a bit of trash on the dusty concrete. He made no effort to greet them, open a door for them, or be sociable in any way.

We're being inspected, thought Jennie. Piece of meat. Playthings.

They pushed the glass doors open and walked into the lobby. Smoke filled the restaurant area. A clerk slowly stood up from a bar stool and walked over to stand behind the reception counter.

"Yeah?"

"Mr. Cross here? We were sent to ... entertain him." Maggie looked at the clerk with no emotion and no more explanation, and waited. He finally nodded, and waved a hand towards the elevator.

"Seven. Turn right, second door."

"Thanks," said Maggie in a flat, don't-let-me-wake-you-up voice, and turned away, squeezing Jennie's elbow and forcing her to turn and move with her. They walked casually to the elevator and pressed the button.

Look bored. Jaded. Probably addicted. How do I do that?

The door opened and two men stood there looking at them. They looked at each other, and back at the women. No one moved.

"You gettin' out?" asked Maggie.

"Maybe," said one. "Come on," said the other as he pushed the first, "I'm hungry." They walked out, and the first man watched the women as he walked by.

"Thanks," said Maggie dully, and walked in. Jennie followed.

"Halfway there!" said Jennie after the door closed. "Think those were his keepers?"

"Yeah, I think that's right. They fit the type. Make my skin crawl. Did you know I've been writing about Leonard and his creeps?"

The elevator crawled up to seven. The door opened on a dreary hall with flickering lights and a carpet that had not been cleaned since the English took up cricket. They turned right and knocked on the second door.

Silence.

After a minute or so, Jennie knocked again, harder, and the door moved. She pushed on it, and they walked in.

Mac awoke in darkness.

He opened his eyes and stared upwards. He was lying on his back, and the stars were brilliant.

The stars?

He watched them for a minute, and realized he had no idea where he was. He lifted up, and immediately fell back down. His back and arm were in pain, as he moved. He lay there quietly, and slowly memory returned. Kidnapped. They thought he knew how the software worked. Thought he had the software. And decided to dump him in the desert, preferably dead.

He rolled to his side and pushed up with the other arm. At first he was dizzy, but after a moment got to his knees, and then up to his feet. Shaky, but standing.

A few feet away lay two men, and he remembered everything. It was time to go home.

Looking up, he searched the sky. Orion... Big dipper ... Little dipper ... Polaris. That way is north. To Mérida, hopefully. Or a road, or the ocean ...

He stumbled over to look at the men. What could he use? Might have a twenty mile walk to get to anywhere, then to Mérida, and would need a flight from there. No idea what time it was ... they had taken everything ... but the bigger man had a watch, and he took it. After three, so about three more hours before the sun came up.

He would need a hat, and the other man would not be needing his. Mac put it on. Loose, but it would work.

Guns? No ... but a machete. Meant for him, as he recalled. They wouldn't be needing that either.

He rolled the smaller man over and stripped his belt off him, and took the belt holster for the machete.

Neither of them had water. How were they ... shouldn't there be a car ... something? That part stubbornly refused to come back to mind, and as he rubbed his hand across the back of his head to brush off the sand, he found a painful place with a swollen lump.

Maybe those memories are in there, he smiled. Maybe they'll come back. But with no water, I'd better get started.

He put on the belt holster and the machete. After making sure there were no water bottles or weapons on the men's bodies, and not seeing a vehicle of any kind nearby, he began walking.

"Star light, star bright ..." he said, trying to get a walking pace started. He stumbled over a rock, and realized he had to be more careful.

I'm in the desert. In the desert, rocks and sand and rattlesnakes go together, and they come out at night... we came on a road, where is it?

By the time the sky turned grey and the heat began to rise, he was miles away along a narrow strip of asphalt, seriously thirsty. Using the machete he sliced up a cactus leaf and got some of the juice from between the spines. He pressed on.

The sun was high when he came to a bigger paved road, and he began walking along it, sweating, stumbling, and watching the asphalt ripple and disappear in the distance.

A truck came rumbling along behind him, and pulled to a stop.

"Amigo. Va á Mérida?"

He looked up at the cab and nodded, too dry and thirsty to speak. Pulling on the handle by the door, he was able to climb up and get the passenger door open. He fell into the seat, reached out, and pulled the door closed. Leaning back, he could not have described the man who had helped him. The truck lurched forward and began picking up speed.

"Norteamericano?"

He nodded again, and looked at the driver. Plaid shirt, well worn white western hat, dirty boots, very faded jeans. An honest working man. A man who was looking at the machete on his belt.

"No problema... hay agua?" he rasped out. "Any water?"

The driver handed him a beer can, cold and full. He ripped off the aluminum tab and drank.

"Gracias." He leaned back, and a minute later had recovered enough to drink the rest of it. "Gracias," he said again.

"Porqué...?" asked the driver, with a wave of his hand at the desert around them.

Thieves. Robbers. What was the word for ... he finally settled on 'bad men'.

"Hombres malos."

The driver nodded, as though that were a fully detailed answer that left no need for any more information. "Á donde?"

Mac motioned with his hand, like a plane taking off. "Airport?"

"Aeropuerto?"

Mac nodded, and laid his head back again. "Sí, por favor, gracias."

The driver laughed, and handed him another beer.

Highway 180 went past the airport entrance, and the driver pulled to the side of the road. He obviously wasn't going to drive the big rig onto airport property, and maybe for reasons Mac couldn't guess.

"Allá," he said, pointing to the sign with the picture of an airplane and the word "Aeropuerto" in the middle of the writing. "Buena suerte."

Mac padded his pockets and said, "No tengo nada. Lo siento."

"No hay problema," the driver shook his head. "Vaya con Dios."

Mac reached over and shook his hand, and stumbled down the steps to the dirt. The truck rumbled away, and he began walking to the terminal that looked ten miles away under a blistering sun.

# Chapter 25

Philip Cross sat in a chair facing the window. He did not move or respond when he heard the knocks on the door. Why should he? More badgering by Leonard, more abuse by his thugs, more desperation and depression. He waited for whatever assault the newest visitors would bring.

"Philip?"

A woman's voice? Who in the world?

He turned and saw a vision from Heaven - Jennie from the college, and someone with her. He stared.

"Philip? Can you speak?"

He stumbled to his feet and croaked, "Can you get me out of here?"

The women looked at each other. "Why not?" said Jennie. The other one shrugged.

Jennie took his arm. "Let's go. Do you need anything?"

"The computer, I guess ..." he waved vaguely towards the laptop on the bed. "But really, just get me out of here!"

Maggie picked up the laptop and they headed for the hall. No one there. Jennie looked around for the stairs furthest from the elevator. "That way. Maybe we can get to an outside door before they realize what's up."

They ran and stumbled and ran. Philip seemed strangely unstable on his feet.

The fire exit door into the stairwell did not want to open, but they spoke to it firmly and convinced it to yield. They pulled it closed behind them and grabbed the rail. The steps descended into darkness; apparently keeping the stairwell lights working was not a priority in Chicago, and apparently safety inspectors did not care about the Plaza.

"Ma'am .. Whoever you are? If you open the laptop, the screen will give us some light ..."

"Sorry. Maggie. Got it." She pulled it open and held it where it would cast at least a little glare downward, and they ran, stumbled, fell, and slid down seven stories.

At the bottom a little light came under the exit door to the hallway, and another door further away looked like an outside exit.

Jennie moved that way.

"Probably set off an alarm," said Maggie.

"Any chance we could go through the lobby and not get taken?"

"None."

"I vote for the alarm," said Jennie grimly, and pushed it open. A loud clanging began.

"Which way is the car?" said Jennie, and Maggie took off running to the left. "Come on!" At the corner she ran across the street to the right. Jennie dragged Philip along. He seemed to be gaining balance and waking up from the dreariness that had enveloped him. Drugs? Probably.

Maggie reached the car and popped the locks open. The car lights blinked. She threw the back door and the passenger door open, and Jennie pushed Philip into the back. A gunshot sounded, and concrete chips flew from the building wall next to them.

"Now! Now!" The women jumped in and slammed doors shut. Maggie rammed it into gear as the rear window shattered. Her tires squealed, and the light in front of them turned red. "Go! You're clear!" shouted Jennie, and they went. The expressway entrance welcomed them, and there were no police to care about that light.

There were, however, people who cared about their escape.

Two cars appeared in the rear view mirror. As Maggie accelerated, Jennie watched in the rear view, and the cars accelerated even faster.

"Hold on," said Maggie. "Cross, keep down!"

Philip dove for the floor in the back, and Jennie slumped down in the front passenger seat. Her outside mirror shattered.

"Nice people!" said Jennie. "These are friends of yours?"

"If they knew who I was, they'd be twice as mad!"

The cars screamed up Lakeshore Drive along Lake Michigan, and Maggie threw it into the exit for Randolph Street. Cars veered away from her on either side as they came off the ramp, and she took two quick turns. At State Street she slammed on the brakes and slid down the wet concrete into a parking garage. Pulling into the first available slot, she shouted "Get out!"

Jennie pulled the back door open and helped a terrified Philip Cross out. They stumbled and ran to the nearest exit door, up the stairs, and into the mall.

"Now," said Maggie, "walk like nothing in the world is happening."

Philip did the worst job, but they all pretended to be as calm as a duck drifting across a pond. Jennie walked by a mall security guard and said quietly, "Call the cops. Some of Leonard's finest are about to blow through here."

He stared as they walked on. Jennie looked back and mouthed the word, "Now!"

They strolled into the department store, found the ladies lingerie section, and stuffed Philip into the fitting room. "Jennie. If someone tries to enter, tell them somebody threw up, and the place is a mess," whispered Maggie. "Start trying stuff on, so we look different than when we walked into the Plaza."

Jennie's phone rang.

"Jennie, where are you?" said Mac.

"Where am I? A Chicago mall, being chased by gangsters. How about you?"

“Nothing that much fun. They dragged me out to enjoy the Yucatán countryside. Not a place where I wanted to spend a lot of time..."

“Any idea why they grabbed you?”

“Yeah. Thought I knew how Cross’ software worked. When they finally realized a Mexican machete knew more than I did, they considered using one on me... and I guess they changed their minds.”

“Did you explain it to them?”

“Sort of. It didn't take long. I’ve got the machete, and they're still out there enjoying the desert. But I'm at the airport. I'll get home when I can.”

She laughed. “Well, I’m proud of you. Listen, I think our goons just walked in. Gotta go.” She hung up, tucked the phone away, and tried to look busy in the swimsuit racks.

“Hey, how long do I need to be in here?” shouted Cross. Sardine Face stopped and looked at her from two aisles over, and mouthed a curse word. “Rock! Paco!” he said softly, and started towards her. She selected a nice aqua string bikini and wandered back towards the fitting room. Maggie came towards her with a lovely red lingerie set.

“What do you think?”

“I would suggest this bikini for Sardine Face - he’s coming from over there ...”

“Great idea. He has friends?”

“He called Rock and Paco.”

“Hmm. May need a little more stuff.” She grabbed a large set of panties.

“Let’s go change.”

They slipped into the changing area. Jennie motioned Cross into one of the stalls and said, “Shut up. You just gave us away.”

He put his hand over his mouth and disappeared into a stall.

Sardine Face stuck his head through the curtain in front of Jennie. She threw her clasped hands straight up into his chin, snapping his head back, then grabbed the front of his shirt and yanked him to the floor inside the stall. She slipped the string bikini around his neck, pulled it tight, and tied the only knot she knew.

Never could untie that darned knot. Maybe he'll have better luck.

"Jen!" came Maggie's voice.

She slipped out the curtain and circled around to the other end of the changing area, picking a nice leather belt off the rack as she went by.

Nice inlays. I'm sure they'll enjoy it.

A man's back was to her, with his head inside the curtain. She looped the belt around his ankles and pulled back as hard as she could. He slammed to the floor and a pistol went off.

I'll skin you, she thought, if you hurt Maggie.

A quick kick to the back of his head, and she stepped over him and through the curtain. Maggie was standing on the bench in the first stall, and the curtain was on the floor. The third man was holding a knife to her belly. Maggie looked at Jennie, and the man turned to see who it was. As he did, Maggie kicked his knife hand and sent the blade flying out of the booth. Jennie threw a kick into his knee, buckling it, and Maggie pulled the large panties over his head.

He struggled to pull them off, but simultaneous punches into his kidneys distracted him, and moments later he was unconscious on the floor, wrapped up and hog-tied in the lovely red lingerie set.

"Beautiful. I always did like that color," said Maggie. "Cross! Time to go!"

He crawled out of the center stall and stared.

"Nice, huh? You should get some training, Philip." Jennie pushed him to the exit, and they followed Maggie out.

Chicago's finest met them. "What's going on here? There was a shot."

“Sam. Good to see you. Maggie, from the Herald.”

He stared. “Uh, right. Hi. What’s up?”

“Three guys in here. Kidnapping, attempted murder, shooting up a vehicle ... running red lights ... the whole list. Some of Leonard’s goons.”

Jennie added, “The one in the far end might survive if you get to him soon.”

Sam motioned one of his men to the other end.

“He’s blue, Sam. Should I get this bikini off him?”

“Of course, Charlie! Take the bikini as evidence, and your wife can have it!” shouted Sam. Turning to Maggie he said, “A bikini?” She shrugged.

“You use what’s handy, sir,” said Jennie.

“Got time to tell us the details, Maggie? Or do you have more of Chicago’s underground to chase?”

“I think that’s all for now, actually. I’d like to show you what’s left of my car, maybe later. I think Leonard will send more of his hit squad after Philip, here. You might give him a little protection.”

“Not likely, unless he wants to be in a jail cell. Could he just leave town?”

“Please,” said Philip. “On the first plane out!”

"Great idea," said Jennie. "Maggie, it's been fun, but I do need to get him home, and I'd like to be home myself when Mac finds his way out of the Yucatán. Let's go!"

The mall security guard ran up. “That’s her, officer, she’s the one!”

Sam looked at him. “Go away.”

# Chapter 26

Philip and Jennie walked into Dr. Sorenson's office unannounced, half an hour before his first class. He stared. Jennie pulled the door closed behind them and locked it.

"Have a seat, Phil. Now. Dr. Sorenson. Did you indeed take $600,000 from Leonard of Chicago and allow him to take Mr. Cross away from the conference hotel?"

"We ... we sold the software. And I had no way of stopping him from taking Phil. Are you OK? Where did he take you?" he asked, turning to Philip.

"Yes, thanks to her. Chicago. The wrong side."

"How did you ... did he send you back?"

Philip shook his head. Jennie waited.

"He tried to kill us."

Sorenson stared again.

"Dr. Sorenson, do you have his money? Can you send it back?"

"But the deal is done! He took Philip, yes, but then Philip showed him the software working!" He leaned back and rubbed his face. "No, I don't have the money. Philip, what happened? You showed it to him. Why did he try to kill you?"

"You remember the joke about the Russian subs? Well, I guessed right. Once."

"Then?"

"Then he paid you, I guess, but then he insisted on predictions, and more, and made some short-term bets ... my track record got pretty poor. I think he lost enough that even he would call it serious money. His guys started making threats. I'm a programmer, not an economics geek, I had no idea what to do. I think I was about to be thrown out a window — with a lot of alcohol in my blood — when the ladies came."

He looked at Jennie. So did Dr. Sorenson, and before "Ladies?" could escape his mouth, she decided to interrupt.

"The cavalry rode in. Not much more to say. But ... how are you going to keep him safe?"

"Him and me both..."

"Philip, how do you get here normally?"

"My car."

"I have a suggestion. Don't ever turn the key in it again."

"Jennie, you can't be serious ..."

"And you, my professor friend, need to be much more careful who you do business with. Now the question on the table is ... what happens next?"

"We go to the police, of course."

"They are very good at cleaning up after the fact. Which in this case would mean finding a good funeral home for the two of you. Next suggestion?"

"I guess we need to rely on you for that answer."

Philip turned to her. "Can I ask a question?"

"Sure."

"What do you do for a living?"

"I teach journalism. Why?"

Mac walked into the Manuel Crescencio Rejón International Airport in Mérida with sweat-soaked clothes, a five-day beard, and serious sunburn.

The United agent looked at him.

"Need a flight home," he said in a dry, raspy voice.

"With that?" She looked at the machete in his hand.

"My carry-on."

She stared, and then laughed. "All right, I give up. Who are you, and what can I do for you?"

"I was kidnapped. I'm desperately hungry, I have no money or clothes, and I need to go home. Type in my frequent flyer number, and we can get started."

She looked past him, and he turned around. Four Mexican officers stood very close. "Can we help you, Señora? Is this man a problem?"

"No, we're fine. He'll be checking the machete."

Apparently unconvinced, none of them moved. He turned back to the agent. "I have a credit card on file. Can I get a flight?"

He picked up his machete - heavily wrapped - at baggage claim and tried to remember where he had left the truck. Then he realized it wouldn't matter. He had no driver's license, no money to pay the garage, and no car keys.

"Taxi! Over here!"

He walked up to the front door and rang the bell. Jennie opened it a moment later and wrapped her arms around him.

"Ma'am?" he said, when he could get a word out, "could you pay this good cabbie something? I, uh ..." he patted his filthy pants ... "I got nothin'."

She laughed, and called to the cabbie, "How much does he owe you? OK, be right back!"

A hot shower, a hot steak, and several hot kisses later, he flopped down on the couch and she flopped down on his lap.

"Do you hurt anywhere?"

"No," he replied, after pretending to check himself over.

"Well," she said, "if you ever do this again..."

"What?!" he exclaimed. "I was kidnapped!"

"I know. I was there. Why did you let them do that? I needed you!"

He laughed. "Sloppy, I know. Careless. Listen, I promise ..."

But those were the last words he got out for a while.

When "Clara" was gone, Andy spent some time cleaning up the taxi. The kidnapping had been rough, and the driver's side of his car had some unwelcome scrapes. He touched up the paint, sprayed sealer on it, and thought about what to do. His pride was irritated. A passenger had been ripped out of his cab, and a friend of his friend had been taken from the hotel.

He practiced assembling and disassembling Mac's rifle, and took it out to the desert several times over the next few days to practice with it.

Nice. Very nice. I really should give it back.

He picked up the phone.

"Carlos? Andy."

"¿Qué pasó, amigo?"

Andy read him the license plate number. "They took my friend. Who are they?"

Carlos left the phone for a minute, then returned.

"You will not like the answer. That car was stolen from the Hertz lot. They found it yesterday at low tide."

"You cannot get out of the Hertz lot without passing the gate and showing ID, right?"

"Unless he's a friend of yours, I guess not. Or you cut the fence."

"Did they?"

"Said nothing about that in the police report..."

"So maybe they have a friend ..."

Andy parked across the street from the exit out of the Hertz lot at the airport. He wandered over to the exit gate, and struck up a conversation with the agent. Almost midnight, not a time when people pick up cars, so things were slow.

"I heard someone stole a car a few days ago."

"Yeah."

"How could they do that?"

Silence, and the agent looked at him more carefully.

"I mean, they have to come past you, right, to get out?"

"Yeah ..."

Andy looked at his name tag. Simón Guerrera. "So, did they?"

"Yeah ... busted right through the gate, and took off." He motioned to the cross-bar. It had a splint nailed to it close to the mechanism that raised and lowered it.

"So they just ran into the bar and broke it?"

"Yeah."

"But there's no damage to the paint..."

The agent looked at the bar where Andy pointed.

"If they rammed it, there would be damaged paint in the middle."

The agent stepped out of the booth and looked closely at the wood, running his fingers along it.

"Guess they painted it."

Andy looked at it again. That was not fresh paint. Whoever broke that bar did not do it by ramming it. He walked over to the splint, and looked at the edges of the bar where the pieces were splinted together. He walked back to the booth.

"Nice watch!"

"Yeah," said Simón Guerrera, "got it last night!"

"Where did you find it? It's gorgeous!"

"Jared's."

"Oh, muy caro también!"

"Yeah, it was pricey. But, hey ... every now and then you gotta splurge, right?"

"Right. So, here's the deal. You tell me who your friends were that stole that car, and I won't tell anyone that you cut that bar for them and took a bribe."

Simón stared at him, and then at his watch. And then at Andy.

"And I want an address, not just a name."

Simón reached into his pants pocket and pulled out a stack of small papers. He flipped through and found a business card, and handed it to Andy.

"If they find out I told you, I'm a dead man."

Andy took the card, memorized the name and address, and handed it back.

"I was never here, and this never happened. Thanks."

He walked back to his car, grabbed some paper from the glove compartment, and wrote down the information.

So, that's the key to the people that took Mr. Cowboy. What about Miss Clara ... he fished her card from his own pocket ... 'Jennie'? What about her friend?

Next morning, he picked up the phone again.

"Carlos? Andy."

"Again?"

"Got him. Found the guy who stole the car. Trade you?"

"For what?"

"Who would an outsider hire to kidnap somebody?"

"You mean, who would an outsider hire to hire somebody to kidnap somebody? So he, personally, would never be caught?"

"Yeah, him."

"Ramón Mir. We can never pin it on him, but he's the guy."

"Any idea where his tough guys hang out?"

"El Toro, mainly, and some over at El Cañón."

"Thanks. Here's the guy who did a free car rental with no return, over at Hertz."

That evening, Andy drove his old pickup down to the drinking part of town. After buying a few drinks for the right people, he ended up meeting a couple of guys that looked right.

"I'm Andy," he said, when the waiter brought beers. "You?"

"Diego."

"Toño."

"You guys do some stuff for Ramón now and then, don't you?"

They looked at each other.

"So what?"

“Like, grab people from a cab and drag them away, sudden like?”

One of the hoodlums took a long drink of his Dos Equis. “Yeah, that could happen." He smiled at his friend. "But last week, whenever it was? On the road to the airport? That wasn't us."

Andy sat back, sipped on his beer, and waited.

"We heard it was three guys, working for some Venezuelan big shot, something about computers. Took him somewhere to find out what he knew."

The man leaned forward. "But only one of them came back. Do you know anything?"

Andy put down his beer and laughed. "I do," he said. "That was my cab. And if they haven't come back ..."

He laughed again. "Bet you dinner anywhere in town, they won't be back. They picked on the wrong guy."

Diego and Toño stared at him. Andy changed the subject.

"But let's talk about you, not them. I think Ramón called, and you went to the Destino. I think you met a gangster, and kidnapped a young man for him. Took him to the airport, stuffed him on a plane to Chicago."

The look on their faces told Andy he was right.

He stood up to leave. "You might want to get out of Mérida. That man they took to the desert? He's going to shut down the guy from Chicago, and if he wants to come find you as well ... it won't be hard."

He left a bill on the table. "That's for the beer, not for you." And he left, as they looked at each other without speaking.

# Chapter 27

Leonard grabbed the phone on the first ring. "Yeah, what?"

"Rock and his guys are in jail. Two women walked into the Plaza, right in the front door, and took the kid. The guys chased 'em, blew out a window, followed them into the mall, and ... it's embarrassing. When the cops got them, they were tied up in women's underwear. Anyway, they're in jail."

"Let them rot."

Slamming the phone down, he took a deep breath, reached into his jacket pocket, and pulled out another cigar.

Can't trust anyone. Send the schmuck to knock off a girl, and she locks him in the trunk of his own car. Stash a college kid in my own hotel, and two women walk him out. My own guys get taken down by ... no. It's her again. It's got to be her again. Who else?

He pulled the phone from his pocket and flipped through the contacts list.

"Jerry. You remember Jennie? Yeah, the prof. Are you man enough to get rid of her?"

"Leonard. This is Jerry. Who do you think you're talkin' to?"

"Then do it. I never want to hear her name again."

He hung up and smiled. Jerry was good. A little messy around the edges, but very, very good. And he lived close to her. He could do it quick.

Jerry put down his scotch. Yeah, he knew Jennie, and she knew him from his varsity year. Wrote about him now and then. The only lady in the press that saw through him.

Be glad to take her down.

Wonder why Leonard is so hot to get rid of her?

He pulled on a Polo shirt and trotted down to the car.

I'll go see her. Drop in to chat, for old times' sake.

Traffic was light, not yet rush hour. He turned into the campus entrance near the quadrangle, and noticed a blonde — short hairdo — driving out. That's her!

OK, let's see where she lives.

He paused in the driveway long enough to see which way she turned, then quickly spun around and got back out into traffic.

Four miles later she turned onto the highway across the lake. The new neighborhoods, further away. OK. He dropped back another quarter mile, confident he could see when she left the road on the other side of the bridge.

Up over the Sentinel, then some farmland... good grief, how far does she drive? At last, she turned into Blossom Creek Village, and he drove on past ... just in case she was noticing him, this would ease her mind. A mile later he turned around, came back, and drove slowly into Blossom Creek. Shouldn't be too hard to find her car in here.

"Honey, are you here?"

"Yeah, in the basement. Welcome home!"

"Come up for a minute."

He trounced up the stairs.

"Come watch. I left the car on the driveway as bait. A blue BMW followed me all the way from the college. Drove past the neighborhood entrance, but I'll bet you a ... there he is!"

They watched as the BMW slowly cruised down their street, paused in front of their house, then rolled on. After a minute it came back by, slowly, from the other direction.

"Jennie, I think your friend in Chicago has put the word out on you. I'm guessing this is a killer."

She looked at him. "What do we do?"

"Set a trap, of course. But we might have to go to Chicago to really put an end to it... and to get him off your friends as well."

The next morning Jerry walked into Jennie's office right after she arrived.

"Yes?"

"Dr.... Or, perhaps I can just call you 'Jennie' now?"

"Jerry?"

"The same."

"Well, it's been a while. Sit down. How are you? Been to Chicago lately?"

He stared. "How did you know I go to ... Chicago?"

"Lucky guess. You look fit. Staying active, I guess. How's the BMW treating you?"

Again, he was speechless. "How did you ...?"

"I'm a journalist. I notice things. What can I do for you?"

"Can I book a lunch with you, just to talk about old times?"

"No, thanks. I'm married." She held up her left hand.

"Oh, nothing romantic," he laughed, "just to talk."

"No, thanks. Anything else I can do for you?"

After a moment of silence, he stood. "No, I guess not. How about you, ever get up to the Windy City?"

"Try to avoid it, truthfully. Some bad memories."

He nodded. "All right, then. Take care."

I will, she thought, as he walked out. I certainly will.

"Can you believe it?" she asked Mac that evening. "Waltzed right into my office, invited me out for chit-chat."

"You accepted, of course."

"Of course, not! Why would I do that?"

"To set a trap. What a great opportunity!"

"With me as the bait! No, thanks ... I saw that movie. It never turns out well for the bait!"

"But, Jen, you ARE the bait. You are who he's after! How do we set a trap without having you in the middle of it?"

She fell back in the recliner. "Aargh."

Her cell phone buzzed the arrival of a message.

*I heard some snakes disappeared in desert. I found two more. Please tell Mr. Cowboy. Is he OK?*

She laughed and relaxed. "Well, some things end well. Here's a note from your taxi driver in Mérida. Looks like they can't find your new friends!"

Mac read it and smiled.

She typed in a reply: *Mr. Cowboy is :-) and OK. Call 4 help if u need it!*

A few minutes later he answered: *OK. Thx.*

"We should bring him up here," mused Mac. "Handy fella."

"Right." She climbed out of the recliner. "I'm tired. Think I'll get ready for bed."

"Yeah, me too. I'll go turn everything off in the basement."

She wandered into the kitchen to reheat her tea, and noticed the full garbage can.

They come early. This has to go out tonight.

She pulled the bag out, tied it, and pushed a new bag down into the plastic can. The timer on the microwave beeped, as she started to the door with the full bag.

Then she paused, set it down, and went to the top of the stairs.

"Mac."

"What's up?" he called, from the other end of the basement.

"I'm about to be the bait. Are you ready?"

"Now you're scaring me!" he said. "Be right there!"

She pushed open the back door and dropped the bag into the

big aluminum can. When she lifted the can to carry it to the street, a strip of duct tape was slapped over her mouth and a cloth sack came down over her head. Someone grabbed her elbows, pulled them behind her back, and threw some tape around them. The trash can fell to the driveway and clattered down the concrete.

"You idiot!" whispered someone, and "Shut up!" was the reply. She was lifted off her feet and her ankles strapped together. They carried her roughly for a few seconds, then dumped her into something. When the trunk lid slammed shut over her, that mystery was solved.

This tape will ruin my makeup, she thought. Good thing I don't use much. Hope Mac gets here soon enough to see which way they go! Couldn't they have taken the spare tire out of here before throwing me in?

# Chapter 28

Mac came trotting up the stairs. "Jen, what is all that racket outside?"

"Jennie?"

He opened the front door, saw the trash spilled all over the driveway, and suddenly knew what had happened. He ran to the street, saw tail-lights rounding the corner in the next block, and cursed.

"Can't a couple just have a nice evening at home anymore?" he muttered. He got on the phone, and opened up the laptop on the kitchen table.

"What is your emergency?"

"My wife was just kidnapped. The car is probably a blue BMW, just now leaving the Blossom Creek Village subdivision."

"Your wife was just kidnapped?"

"Yes, can we move a little quicker please?"

"What is your name, sir?"

"All right, look, I don't have time for twenty questions. I'm going to chase them until you get there. Tell the police what I just told you! Here's the number they can reach me on." He hung up, logged into Jennie's iCloud account and hit the "Find my iPhone" utility. While the blue dot wandered across the map, he threw a few things into a bag and changed shoes.

Ten minutes later the dot settled in on a desolate area south of the lake. He took a screen shot, pushed it to the printer, and locked the door behind him.

The roads turned to gravel and dirt before he reached the house. He drove slowly with the lights off, trying not to raise any dust in the dim moonlight. He came around a corner and saw it; three cars outside, lights in the bottom, dark upstairs. He pulled off the road and nestled the truck into the brush. Putting his phone on silent and pulling a black cap down over his head, he checked the flashlight and began walking across the rough unmowed field surrounding the house.

The phone vibrated. He pulled it out. Did not recognize the number.

"Yes," he said quietly.

"Police. Your wife has been kidnapped?"

"They took her to Manor Road, about ten miles south of the city, a two story house in the middle of a field, three cars. I'm going in. Be discreet."

He hung up. Hope that was all they needed.

As he moved silently towards the house, he spotted a blue BMW. He memorized the license plate, but realized there was no need ... they knew who owned it. But it might help the police. While he was at it, he memorized the plates on the other two cars as well.

No one on guard?

He smelled a cigarette being smoked. Easing up to the wall of the house, he worked his way down the near side, past some flowerpots and lawn chairs, and at the corner the smoke was stronger. He stooped down as close to the ground as he could get, eased his head barely around the corner, and almost jumped when the person sitting in a chair close to his head spoke.

"How long you think it'll take him?"

"Not long," said another voice on the other side of the speaker. "He doesn't really care what she's gonna tell him, he's just playing with her before we get rid of her. The boss didn't want anything, just to be rid of her."

Another bright glow of a cigarette being drawn, and a long

puff of smoke out into the moonlight.

Mac felt around on the ground for something he could throw, and tossed a clump of dirt as far into the darkness past the men as he could without making a sound.

"You hear that?"

"Yeah. Raccoons in the garden, probably. They come out at night. Eat anything they find."

He tossed another bit of gravel.

"That ain't coons. He got dogs here?"

"It ain't dogs. You'd hear 'em diggin' and barkin', if dogs were chasin' somethin' out there."

"Well, I'm gonna go look, see what it is."

"Fine, you go."

As the other man stood up, scraping his chair on the concrete, Mac stood up, using that noise to cover his movement. The near man took another long draw on the cigarette. As he did, Mac stepped around the corner, and threw a straight-hand chop three inches under the glow of the cigarette. The seated man grunted and slumped forward.

"What was that?" called his friend from out in the yard.

"Smoke..." said Mac, and coughed a couple of times.

"Careful, man, those cancer sticks'll kill you."

"Yeah," said Mac roughly, and slipped past the man in the chair. He found the door into the house and quickly opened it, slipped in, and pulled it closed behind him, locking it.

The gamble worked. No one was in the kitchen he had entered. Voices came from the living room.

"So, what did you do to make the old man so upset?"

Sounded like someone stretched out on a couch, not someone standing up. Someone completely relaxed and lazy.

"Same thing I'm going to do to you."

"Excuse me? You are tied up like a cow in a rodeo, and you're gonna do what to me?"

Mac slipped his phone out and pressed her contact listing. He put his phone back in his pocket, and heard hers ringing as it did only when he called her.

"Excuse me, can we take a break from this fascinating conversation? I need to take this call."

The man laughed. "You got minutes to live before I dump you in a ditch somewhere, and you want to take a call?" He laughed again. "Here, I'll take your stupid call! Since you can't move your hands and all!"

Mac heard him get up from wherever he was sitting.

What can I use ...

He picked a frying pan off the stove.

"Whaddya want?"

Mac stepped into the room and swung the pan, catching the man across the front of the head as he stood with his back to Jennie. He fell across the floor and rolled to a stop, not moving.

"That was me calling. Just checking up on you."

He took three strides to the front door, locked it, and came back with a pocket knife open. "Let's get you out of here!"

When the tape was removed, he grabbed her cell phone from the floor, put her at the front door and turned off all the light switches he could find.

"The ground is rough. We've got a hundred yards or so, out the front and angle off to the right. Stay low and quiet. One guy is in the back, and he'll come after us about ..."

They heard someone trying to open the back door.

"... now."

They slipped out the front door, and Mac locked it again behind them.

"Between those cars and off to the right. Behind that oak, there." He pointed.

"Got it," she whispered.

As they ran, the other man came around the house shouting names, then rattled the front door. "Why are the doors locked? Open up!" he shouted.

When Mac and Jennie slipped into the truck and eased out onto the road, the man was still shouting at the locked house. "That's Jerry, inside," she said. "Pity you didn't get to chat with him."

"We should disappear," Mac said. "He'll follow us. Ever been to Mérida?"

"Once," she said, leaning over to kiss him. "Nice place. Didn't really have time to enjoy it."

"I've got a friend there, and he may be able to help. You busy?"

"I could take off a few days," she said.

"Then, I was thinking we might go to Chicago."

# Chapter 29

As the plane settled onto the runway, Mac turned his cell phone back on.

"Andy. This is Mr. Cowboy."

"Mr. Cowboy, sir, where are you? Back in my beautiful city with one less boa constrictor?"

"The very one, and I brought Miss Clara with me. Can you meet us at the airport?"

"You are my next customer, Mr. Cowboy, sir!"

As they walked through baggage claim, two boys met them with a sign that said, "Mr. Cowboy."

"Well, this is a surprise," said Mac. "Who are you?"

"Carlos, sir, and my brother, Javier."

"And ... you know my name, because ..."

"Papi sent us to carry your bags, Señor Cowboy, sir. Hello, Miss Clara, ma'am!"

Jennie laughed. "Hello, my friends! We don't have enough money to tip both of you! Maybe we could buy you a milkshake instead?"

"Yes, ma'am!" they both answered at once.

At the cab, the boys piled into the front with Andy, and Mac and Jennie relaxed into the back.

"Where to?"

"Thought maybe you could suggest someplace, and have dinner with us."

"Norteño music OK?"

"Surprise us."

They pulled up at the Venado Loco nightclub, and Andy came around to open Jennie's door. "Need to get these young gentlemen home, but you'll see them again. Be back in seventeen minutes. Tell Marcos that you want to be at Cabby's table, and Cabby will have a serious beer."

Marcos seated them near the little stage and against the far wall, just out of the lights. They could see everything in the place, and could hardly be seen themselves.

"Thinks like I do," said Mac. "Appetizer?"

"Anything with cheese," said Jennie. "Have I ever told you my favorite food is cheese *au gratin*? Here ... *chile con queso!*"

Andy slipped into the other chair seventeen minutes later, with his cold beer waiting on the table.

"So, you found the man who told them to grab me out of your cab?"

"One of them, Mr. Cowboy. Found the car. It was stolen from Hertz. The guard got a nice watch, for helping! But I found who stole it, and gave that to the police. They said he won't be around anymore, but ... who hired him ... don't know."

"Somebody told them I knew all about the magic software, so they grabbed me." He looked at Jennie, and winked. "Popeye."

"Really!" she said. "I shouldn't have been so nice to him when I found him in your room!"

Mac looked at Andy and shook his head. "You know her better than that!"

Andy laughed. "Miss Clara, you had me ... !"

"Andy," said Mac, "we think the man who kidnapped Mr. Cross is trying to kill Miss Clara."

"¡Qué cosa! You do get some attention!" said Andy, and put down his beer. "What we do now?"

"If a Mr. Jerry comes after me here, we deal with him. If we have to go deeper, we go to Chicago."

"I know Chicago. Bought a lot of stuff there, for sale here. To the tourists, you know, who want native stuff. I can speak real English if you need me to!"

"You are a new surprise every day, Andy," laughed Jennie. "Great. We have a team. What about your boys?"

"Young, but smart. Good jiu-jitsu training. Ready to help. They don't look dangerous, so ... bam! Surprise." He picked up the beer again. "So... we set a trap for Señor Jerry?"

"Yes... let's have Miss Clara check in at a big hotel, using her real name ... the one Mr. Jerry will know ... and expect him to try to break into her room. By the way, Andy, you have a passport, right? No problem flying?"

The next morning, the boys were playing chess in the hotel lobby.

"Javier, you can't put your queen there. She has to ..."

"I know, I know," said the younger boy. "Just seeing if you would notice."

Carlos waited, his pieces all centered on exactly the right squares. "You got the goop to put on the floor?"

"Yes," said Javier, not looking up from the board. "If the castles were really rocket ships, and the knights were the pilots, then the bishops could be ..."

"Javier. Could we just play chess?"

"Bo ... ring. OK. You go first."

"But you're playing the white pieces."

"So?"

"White always starts."

"Here," said Javier, spinning the board around. "Now go first."

Carlos shook his head, and moved a pawn out.

"Can we play that Queens can jump over other players?"

"No, Javier, Queens cannot jump over other players."

"But it would be more interesting if ..."

"Your move."

"OK, OK... there." A knight appeared in front of the pawns.

"Wait ... that's not part of this set. You've got three knights. Where did that come from?"

"The table over there." Javier pointed. "They were done with it."

"Javier. Give them their knight back, and play one of your own."

"Awww."

"Here he comes," whispered Carlos, when Javier sat back down. "When I say 'now', throw the stuff on the floor."

Javier nodded, and studied the board.

"Now."

Jerry found her the next morning at the Destino, sipping coffee at a small table in the lobby.

He walked quietly up behind her, and just before reaching her table found himself falling hard on the marble floor. He rolled onto his side with a groan and looked for what had tripped him. Two boys looked down from their chess game.

"Sir? The floor is wet, see the sign?"

Jennie stood over him. "Well, Jerry, what a surprise seeing you here! Wow, that's a nasty bruise. Excuse me, gotta go." She stepped around him and walked briskly out of the restaurant.

He cursed, pushed himself up, and stood. The boys were gone as well, one of their kings tipped over on the board, but hardly any other pieces moved.

"Pretty early in the game to forfeit ..." he thought dully.

He dusted off and hurried out into the lobby. No sign of her. Out front? No... back to her room?

"Excuse me, my sister has checked in. Can you tell me her room number?"

The clerk believed him and looked it up. Jerry headed for the elevator. Third floor. As he came out of the elevator, he looked for a sign showing which way to go, and suddenly was on the floor again, face down, hard.

"Excuse me, sir, in a hurry."

He looked around in time to see the elevator door closing, but whoever was in it was off to the side... sounded like that same kid!

Muttering, he got to his hands and knees, and pushed up to standing. OK, which way to that room...?

He knocked on Jennie's door and said, "Room Service."

The door was propped slightly open, and a voice said, "Come in."

He pushed it open and found a rifle barrel pointed at his chest.

"Come in, Mr. Jerry. Hands up."

He lifted his hands and took three slow steps in, wondering who this could be, this short person with a rifle who knew his name.

"On your knees beside the bed."

He knelt down, hands still raised. Jennie and a man sat at the table playing cards. The short man moved to the door, sat down with his back against it, and held the rifle pointed at Jerry's chest.

No one spoke to him.

"Got any perch?" said Jennie.

"Go fish."

"Excuse me..." said Jerry.

"You're excused," said the man, without looking. "Got any bass?"

"Nope," said Jennie. "Got any sharks?"

"One," said the man. "There by the bed."

Jennie turned and looked at Jerry.

She turned back to Mac. "You're right. But you need four."

"I'll bet he could lead us to three more..."

"You know, I'll bet he could. How could we persuade him to do that?"

"Hmm. If he's willing to kill you ... and that seems to be why he came ..."

"Wait a minute!" said Jerry. "Why do you..."

"... Then I'll bet he's killed others. Can we find out who?"

"No problem. I've found five already, and that's just in the last two years!" Jennie looked at him and smiled.

Jerry stared. How could she ...

"Right, Jerry? How many more do I need to find, to have the whole list?"

"Was he charged for any of these?" asked the man at the table.

"Not yet. But I think I can get him charged for at least three, with what I know now. And I'm not done."

"Jennie, you amaze me. You're really good."

"I know."

The short man at the door laughed, but the rifle never moved.

"So you think he would lead us to the big fish, in exchange for not facing murder charges?"

"Depends. Would the big fish eat him alive?"

"Yeah ... so we should just kill him now."

"No ..." protested Jerry. "I'll ..."

"You'll what?" asked the man, suddenly very attentive.

The room was silent.

Jerry realized he was not sure what he would do ... what he could do ... whether he was in more danger from these people or from Leonard. He knew what Leonard would do, but he was not sure what these people would do ...

# Chapter 30

As they walked off the plane at gate H14 in the O'Hare airport, Jerry asked, "So what is that thing in my back? And how did I get through the scanner?"

"You ask a lot of questions. I'm the journalist. Just do right, and it won't matter." She steered them to the Starbucks at H6.

Cups in hand, Mac followed behind as they trudged to the Hertz counter.

"SUV, sporty please?"

Slot 223 had exactly what she wanted, and they pulled out onto I-90.

"Nice night for a drive," she commented, rolling her window down.

"You'll mess my hair!" complained Mac.

"If you had any..." she replied, and rolled his window down too.

Jerry reached up from the back seat and hooked an elbow around Jennie's neck. "Dying in a wreck might be the best thing for me, so I don't care if we crash. Get over to the surface road and let me out!"

"Sorry you feel that way, old man," said Mac. "Maybe I can help you."

Suddenly Jerry fell back, screaming. After ten seconds he suddenly stopped, and lay in the back groaning.

"What took you so long?" asked Jennie. "I may need a chiropractor!"

"Sorry. Thought he had better manners. Now I know better."

Mac turned to look at Jerry. "Any more requests? Any more questions about that thing in your back?"

Nothing more was said until they reached the Plaza.

"We're stopping here?" said Mac. "You sure?"

"Yes, unfortunately," said Jennie. "The freeway entrance is just there," she pointed, "in case it matters. Here are the keys... I think you might be the one who needs them. And, lock it ... or my guess is it'll be stolen about the time we get inside the main doors!"

Mac looked around and nodded.

"What are we doing?" asked Jerry.

"You're taking us to Leonard. That simple. Got it?"

"He'll be furious! He's in bed by now, and rages when someone wakes him!"

"Have you ever seen Jennie in a rage, my friend?" asked Mac. "Your choice."

Jerry looked back and forth between them, and shrugged. "As long as you go in first..."

"No, I think we get to manage the parade," said Jennie. "Or we throw your pet collar into 'lock' and leave town."

There was no competition for the illegal parking spot right in front of the building, and as they walked up the stairs it was close to midnight.

"Nice night to check into a luxury hotel," said Jennie.

"I thought we might just visit ... check out the accommodations ... then maybe stay somewhere a little more in line with our budget?" suggested Mac. She smiled at him.

"When we're done, this place might suit us just fine," she replied. Looking around, she added, "Or maybe not. Moldy."

The main doors swung wide at a touch, though they squeaked a bit, and no one was in the lobby. Jennie looked at Jerry.

"24," he said, and pointed to the elevator.

"Where's the electrical room?" asked Mac.

Jerry looked around. "There's a mail room downstairs, maybe they are together."

“Let’s go see,” suggested Jennie, motioning towards a stairway. Jerry led the way.

The downstairs lights were out.

“No emergency lights?” asked Mac. Jerry shrugged and kept walking.

Mac turned on a flashlight. “Boy Scouts to the rescue.”

Jennie tried the door marked ‘Mechanical’ and could not open it.

“Not locked,” said Jerry. He kicked the handle and it flipped up as the door eased open. “Never used.”

Mac stuck his head in, then disappeared into the utility closet. Jerry took off running. Four steps later he fell to the floor, grimacing.

“Thanks for not screaming, that was a good choice,” said Jennie. “Did you think only Mac could pull the trigger on you?”

Mac looked out. “Is he being a problem?”

“No,” groaned Jerry from the floor, “he’s not a problem.”

“What do you see?” she asked.

“Want to shut down power to the 24th floor?”

“I think that’s a peachy idea. Go ahead.”

A loud clank later, Mac came out.

“Jerry, buddy, old friend, which stairwell is the boss going to come down?”

Jerry wobbled a bit as he got to his feet. “Can we go back to the lobby?”

In front of the reception desk, Jerry pointed to the far west end of the hallway. “Maybe there.”

They walked to that stairwell, and opened the door. Shouts and curses were coming from higher up.

“Sounds like our man. What happens when he comes out? You know he won’t be dressed for an evening out...”

“You know what they say,” laughed Jennie. “‘You can dress them up, but you can’t take them out’ ... I think we have the other problem here. But let’s offer him a night on the town anyway.”

"How about if I bring the car around to here?" asked Mac. "More convenient, you know."

"Sure. Twenty-four flights in total darkness... I think you could wait until dawn, and still beat him here."

"Five minutes."

"Go."

Four minutes and thirty seconds later, stumbling steps and profanity grew loud and the door burst open. Leonard stood there in his bathrobe, with two wheezing men behind him who tumbled out through the door and fell onto the ground. Leonard stared at Jerry and Jennie.

"I told you ... what in blazes ... how did she ..." Leonard sputtered, and Jerry offered no comment.

"I'm going to ..." Leonard began towards Jennie. She pointed at Jerry and he screamed, collapsing on the tile floor. Leonard stopped. She dropped her hand, and Jerry stopped screaming, but groaned and whimpered on his knees.

"Shall I do that to you?" she asked Leonard.

"You can't."

She raised a hand towards him.

"No, stop, don't," he shouted, and backed up against the wall.

She waved her hand at the men on the floor. "On your faces, please." They were quick to obey, staring at Jerry.

Mac opened the door to the outside, and Jennie motioned to Leonard. "Out."

He walked sideways, still facing Jennie, and eased out the door as Mac held it open.

"You, too," she said to Jerry. "The rest of you guys stay here."

Jerry struggled to his feet and quickly followed Leonard.

"Hands against the wall, Leonard," said Mac as they all got outside, and he pushed the older man to the wall when he hesitated. In a moment Mac reached down the back of Leonard's bathrobe and slapped an adhesive patch between his shoulder blades.

"Shall I test it, Leonard, or will you trust me that it works?"

He growled, but added, "No, I'm fine."

"Let's let them drive, Jennie, what do you think? We can snuggle in the back seat."

"Nice. I like it. Full moon out? Nice night for a long walk on a Lake Michigan pier?"

"Maybe," said Mac. "Maybe." He tossed the keys to Jerry. "Lakeshore Drive, if you don't mind? South."

A car came around the corner at the other end of the block and parked. Jennie and Mac looked at each other. "Company?"

They slipped into the back seat as Jerry took the wheel and Leonard climbed into the passenger seat, clutching his bathrobe tighter and clicking the seatbelt in place. "You will regret this," Leonard muttered.

"I feel a need to test Leonard's collar," said Mac.

"No, don't start him screaming, it would be unpleasant. Unless he misbehaves, of course."

"Of course."

As they drove away, Jennie struck up a casual conversation with Leonard.

"So, Leonard, now that we have a few minutes to chat..."

"I'll get you. I'll get you fast and hard. You are dead meat."

"Yeah, I like you too, big boy, but here's the question... how can I persuade you to leave me alone, and to leave my friends alone?"

"Like Cross and 'Doc'?"

"'Doc'? Is that what he called himself?"

"Yeah. He owes me."

"How much?"

"Six hundred big ones, and my pride."

"Well, you sent Mr. Jerry here to kill me, so you owe me more. Do I collect?"

There was silence in the car.

"Like... what do you mean, 'collect'?"

"You sent him to rub me out. Capisci? So, do I rub you out?"

"No, I mean, I mean... No."

"How can I persuade you to get out of my life, no matter what happens?"

"No matter what? That's a big order, lady, and there's no telling what might happen?"

"Yeah, I might testify ... the Larkin case, for example, or the bank fraud up in Milwaukee?"

Leonard spun around in the seat belt and stared at her with eyes squinting. "What do you know about those?"

Jennie yawned. "What does ... let's see, who is there you haven't bought already... what does the federal judge in Champagne-Urbana know, that's probably a better question."

Leonard smiled, and turned back around.

"Bad news," said Mac. "He's already bought every judge in the state. We should just shoot him. Lots of people would thank us."

"No! " came the protest from the front seat.

# Chapter 31

Andy watched Mac and Jennie take their hostage into the outbound plane, and worried. Jerry was not bound in any way, and that electronic thing might be confiscated.

Could they get through Customs with it?

He packed light. Small tools for whatever might need doing, a few clothes, a flashlight. Get it all in a backpack, a carry-on, nothing checked in luggage.

An hour later he was on the next flight to Chicago, trying to sleep. Didn't expect much sleep when he got there.

He rented a cheap, small car from an off-brand company and drove to the south side. Didn't know if Mr. Cowboy and Miss Clara got here with any firepower, but he was uncomfortable being in one of the most dangerous cities in the world without gunpowder and a barrel. Didn't take long to find a small .45 that didn't require any paperwork. With a couple boxes of shells in the backpack and an IWB holster over his right kidney he felt much better prepared to see the town.

His cell phone buzzed. A street address ... must be Leonard's building. He touched it, and the map popped up showing its location. "Directions to here" ... from "Current Location" ... duck soup. He found the next freeway entrance and headed that way.

When he came around the corner, he saw them getting into the SUV. But they were in the back?

The car pulled away, and he followed close enough to not get separated.

"Where we going?" said Jerry.

"Jerry, my friend, there's a short pier that goes out over the water, down by the museum, comes out from the yacht club ... do you know it?"

Jerry laughed.

"Mac, I think he knows it very well. I think we've picked just the spot."

Jerry did not laugh again. "Are we being followed?" he said.

"Hope so," said Jennie. "I hate small parties."

Jerry pulled off Lakeshore, curved around, and turned into the small parking area at the entrance to the pier.

"Keys, please," said Mac.

Jerry turned off the car and handed them over his shoulder.

"Out, please."

All four doors opened, and when Jerry turned around, Mac's 45 calibre XD was pointed at him.

"Walk." Mac stepped back and nodded toward the pier.

"You, too," said Jennie, as Leonard pulled himself out.

Jerry walked past the car. Leonard pulled his bathrobe tighter and came to walk beside him. "It's freezing out here. I'll have your neck! You were supposed to ..."

Mac interrupted. "Jennie, is this pier long enough?"

"He can't swim," she said. "People like him never can."

"What are you talking about?" demanded Leonard.

A small car pulled up next to theirs and stopped with the engine still running. The driver's window rolled down, but nothing was said.

"Wait here," said Mac to the open window. "If we don't come back, make sure no one else does either." There was no answer. As they followed Jerry and Leonard out onto the pier, the small car pulled ahead to block the entrance to the pier and turned off its motor.

They walked slowly out onto the pier.

"OK, we're here," said Jerry, turning around. "Now what?"

A jolt hit his back, and he stumbled.

"Please continue," said Jennie. "And throw your phone out into the lake. And your wallet, too, for that matter."

Jerry cursed, and dumped his pockets over the side of the pier into Lake Michigan. They walked to the end of the pier, and turned around. Mac and Jennie stopped about ten yards back, and the green dot from the laser on Mac's automatic was dancing on Leonard's white robe.

"Stop that!" said Leonard.

"Here's the deal, Leonard," said Mac quietly. "You are one trigger pull away from dead. You have killed people, and had people killed, and you have been trying to kill my wife."

"True?"

There was no answer. Mac raised the pistol to eye level, at arm's length, with the other hand bracing it for use. The green dot bounced back and forth between Leonard's eyes.

"Yes!" blurted out Jerry, and Leonard stared at him.

"You will get somebody on a plane tomorrow. At noon the next day they will meet Philip at the front door of Jennie's school, and that person will go fix Philip's car — if it needs to be fixed — and sit in it, and turn the key."

There was no response.

"And you will never leave this state again. Ever."

Leonard started to object.

"You will say goodbye to that money," he continued, "and both of you will leave us and our friends alone. Forever."

"Or what?" snarled Leonard.

"Or I will publish everything I know about you," said Jennie. "In fact, I've already given the package to two other people, in case anything happens to us."

"And what I know about you," she added, looking at Jerry.

They waited. Jerry looked at Leonard, and Leonard stared at the gun.

"Do we have a deal?" said Mac. "Or do you each take a bullet in the chest now, and float out on the lake together?"

Leonard tried to speak, but he seemed to be having a little trouble getting the words out.

"Jennie," said Mac. "We should just do this. The police in this town will throw a party for us!"

"I agree," said Jennie. "Go ahead."

Mac pulled the trigger. Gunpowder exploded, the firearm kicked back, and a .45 calibre hollow-point shell flew between Leonard and Jerry, head high.

"All right, all right!" screamed Leonard.

"Good. Now lie down," said Mac. "Face down. Now."

Both men fell to the pier, sprawled out on their faces. Mac motioned to Jennie, and they walked back to the waiting car. The window rolled down.

"We're done, Andy. Thanks. Let's go home. See you at the airport!"

At nine the next morning, Philip and Dr. Sorenson came to the conference room near Jennie's office.

Mac, Jennie, and Andy stood to greet them. Mac closed the door behind them, and stood with his back against it. Andy walked over and joined him. Neither of them spoke.

"My partners," said Jennie, waving at them. "Mac and Andy. Mac, this is Dr. Sorenson, and ... do you already know Philip Cross? No, I guess not. Please sit down, everyone."

Mac began. "Philip, tomorrow at noon you will meet Leonard, or someone he sends, at the main door."

"What?" exclaimed Philip, standing up. "No ..."

"He will ask for the key to your car. Give it to him, and take him to your car. You have not used it again, have you?"

"She said not to."

"He will take the key, open the car, get in, and turn the key. He might need to work on the engine or something first."

"And ... " Philip slowly sat back down.

"I would suggest standing at least fifty yards away. And shooing away anyone else who comes close. If he starts the car and nothing happens, get your keys back and he'll leave. If they've hot-wired the car, and he doesn't get it fixed, just wait for the police and tell them who he was and what just happened."

Philip stared at him. "Who he was?"

Mac nodded.

"And... me?" Asked Dr. Sorenson.

"Does he know your name?" asked Jennie.

"Sorenson thought for a moment. "All he had from me was a phone number, and the bank routing information. Maybe not? ... unless Philip told him."

Philip shook his head.

"He could find you from that, but maybe you'll be OK. I'm holding some things over his head."

Before Sorenson could ask the question that ran across his face, Mac continued.

"Philip, we will be close by. If anything unexpected happens, you won't need to deal with whoever comes. And you really don't need to speak to them at all. Just hand over the keys and point to the car."

Philip nodded. "Thank you."

Jennie glanced at her phone, then looked at it more carefully. "Mac, look at this."

He looked over her shoulder.

"It's from Celena. '*The goose lays pretty eggs, but can't fly.*' She's in Venezuela, I think. What does this mean?"

"Hmm. Goose, pretty eggs. Golden goose. Golden eggs. Valuable answers... the software works?"

Jennie laughed. "How many times will this albatross try to be a goose?"

"Who can't fly? Her, or the goose?"

"I don't know. Someone must be seeing her messages. This is cryptic on purpose."

"I think she's being held against her will," said Mac. "The conversation has to look... like it's about birds. Tell her we can come."

"Northern geese can," Jennie typed.

"OK, she understood. But we need to know where she is."

"Ask where the goose builds its nest. The goose she's talking about."

The answer came back: *"The school knows."*

"Tell her we're coming," said Mac.

"But for us ... it's over?" asked Sorenson.

"I think so," said Jennie, standing up. "But if you guys can quit trying to get yourselves killed, the rest of us would appreciate it!"

www.ingramcontent.com/pod-product-compliance
Lightning Source LLC
Chambersburg PA
CBHW070320190726
48291CB00014B/2476

* 9 7 8 1 9 3 7 9 7 5 2 7 2 *